Ghosts of the

Opera

Parisian Ghosts

Janna Ruth

ISBN: 978-1-0670001-3-4 (eBook)

ISBN: 978-1-0670001-4-1 (Paperback)

PARISIAN GHOSTS 4

GHOSTS OF THE OPERA

JANNA RUTH

A NOTE ON SENSITIVE TOPICS

D ear Reader,

This is a book about ghosts, so naturally death plays a rather large part. If you don't like spoilers, and you're cool with everything, skip this note and start the book. If you want to be prepared, read on. I'm writing this because reading should be fun, not a nasty surprise.

In this book, Alix gets swept up in a murder mystery that includes feuding divas and clinically insane ghosts. If you've ever read or watched the Phantom of the Opera, you'll know what horrors may be unleashed.

She's also sort of on the run from the ghost police, keeping a very important secret. She suffers some physical violence in the later part of the book and revisits her drowning trauma once more.

In addition to that, there are mentions of drug abuse in someone's past and a deadly accident. Allusions to Sébastien's ghost whisperer creation and death by electrocution are made throughout the book as Alix gets to know him better.

The series is full of action with physical confrontations between the living and the dead, but our heroine is scrappy and will gain some strong supporters along the way.

Happy to tag along? Then join Alix in this new ghostly adventure on the streets of Paris!

Love, Janna

Grab your free copy

When an undead movie star asks you for a small favour, you know you're gonna be in deep trouble.

Seeing ghosts is just something I've learnt to live with. They're everywhere I go, especially since I chose to study history at the Sorbonne, one of the oldest universities in the world. While on a class trip to the Pantheon, where France's great men—and women!—reside, I get introduced to the fabulous Josephine Baker! One of her war medals has gone missing, and she wants me to find its whereabouts.

Who could say no to a flapper girl turned movie star turned war hero? Little do I know agreeing to do so will send me on a wild-goose chase across the country with a ghostly pet cheetah, hidden walkways, and a murder attempt.

Follow Alix on her first big ghost adventure two years prior to the events of Parisian Ghosts.

Sign up to my Story Seeker mailing list at www.janna-ruth.com/ newsletter and grab the prequel for free

CHAPTER 1

"I need your help. If all else fails, I need you to be my eyes."

Blinking, I stare at Sébastien. My brain's trying to make sense of what's happening. The fact that Petite Alix is unharmed and well. Or that he's in my room. And most importantly, that he wants my help.

For the last couple of days, I've been in absolute agony, thinking I'd lost my ability to see and talk to ghosts. After GoPol led a raid into the catacombs and arrested me, they took Petite Alix from me, scheduling her destruction. And yet, she's here. In Sébastien's arms.

Unable to find any words just yet, I get out of bed, wave him into my room, and close the door behind him. I'm well aware I'm wearing nothing but pyjamas—and short ones at that—my hair looks like a rat's nest, and my eyes are likely more red than white after days of non-stop crying.

I still don't know what to say when my gaze falls on Petite Alix. The little girl is just as unsure as me about what's happening. Her eyes are wide and full of recent terrors. I decide then that Sébastien can wait, crouch in front of her, and stretch out my arms. "Come here."

Sébastien lets go of her hand and she practically falls into my embrace. Shaking like the leaves of a tree in a gust, she digs her little fingers into my pyjama top and buries her face in my chest. There's no crying this time, and if anything, that terrifies me even more.

"Ssh, ssh. You're safe now." I look up at Sébastien, wanting him to confirm it.

He swallows—not a good sign. But then he clears his throat. "For now, she should be safe. It was my task to... *remove* her. I ran the process and put in the report, but I kept her safe in a cupboard, then took her out as soon as the coast was clear. To the best of my father's knowledge, she's gone, and you're no longer a ghost whisperer." His voice makes it very clear I need to remember that.

It's probably really important, but all it does is confirm I'm still a ghost whisperer. Which begs the question, where the hell did Gaspar go? He was with me that first night back home, but in the morning, he was gone, leaving me to believe I'd lost him and all the rest of my ghosts.

I pick up Petite Alix and gently rock her on my hip. "So, you lied."

Sébastien looks mighty uncomfortable. "Yes."

"Does that... does that mean you went rogue too?" As different as they seem, I have to remember he and Dix *are* the same person.

He instantly deflates and I realise I've hit a sore spot. "I... Look, I don't know what's going on with Dix, but I can't lose him. And I don't agree with robbing you of your talents either. You've got a way with ghosts no one else does. It's something to explore, not steal."

"Your father thinks I'm a security risk," I say carefully.

Sébastien winces. "That's what he said about Dix too. He told me Dix attacked his ghost and has been going behind my back."

I hate to break it to him, but... "He has."

There's no shock on his face, just bitter resignation. "I figured as much."

"Well, I'm glad to hear he made it out. Last time I saw him, your father's ghost gave him a thrashing." My stomach turns just thinking about it.

Sébastien frowns. "Wait. You were there?"

"Oh boy." Petite Alix is starting to get heavy, so I carry her over to Malou's cage and give her a little attention. "Would you like to play with Malou?"

She nods, keeping quiet otherwise. I put her on the floor and open Malou's cage. Since it's only four in the afternoon, the little hedgehog is still a bit sleepy, but she doesn't mind me picking her up. Petite Alix puts her little hands together, and I carefully place

Malou on them. Her entire focus is on the hedgehog in her lap as she softly strokes her spikes.

Happy to leave them alone for now, I return to Sébastien. "Why did you decide to come here of all places?" Last time I saw him, he'd held me down in the raid. And before that I'd torn into him with the intention to inflict as much pain as possible. We don't exactly have the best track record.

He's still standing awkwardly in my room, not even sure where to look. "I told you. Dix went rogue. If they take my powers away, I need your eyes."

I cock my head. "Why mine, though? I thought I was persona non grata at GoPol. Especially after the stunt I pulled at the party."

"Oh, you are." He cracks the smallest of smiles. "That was quite impressive. I don't think anyone's ever stolen a ghost from GoPol."

"You just did."

He sucks in his lips and nods. "Yeah, there's that." He looks around. "Can I...?"

"Sit? Sure." I offer him my desk chair and lean against my wardrobe, hands behind my back as I watch him carefully. "I guess, the real question is, are you aware that coming to me will make you a traitor as well?"

"I'm not stupid. If my father learns I've disobeyed his orders, he'll flay me alive. I don't like it."

"Then why are you here?"

He finally meets my eyes. "Because it beats the alternative."

"The alternative?"

His voice hardens as he explains, "My father's plan is as follows: find Dix and eliminate him. And once that's dealt with, he'll make me another ghost. You know what that means."

Unfortunately, I do. "So, you don't want to be murdered again?"

"Is that a rhetorical question?" Sébastien rolls his eyes slightly, but he's loosened up a bit, which was all I wanted to achieve.

"How did you figure it out?" he asks, since I confronted him with the knowledge at the party. I also said a lot of other horrible stuff, like how he deserved the abuse he'd experienced.

I take a deep breath. "In a way, I suppose I knew ever since you explained how ghosts were made. I didn't want to acknowledge it, though, because who does that? Who's so obsessed with their work they'd sacrifice their own child? I thought maybe you did it yourself to please him, but you wouldn't have been able to control the outcome. In the end, Dix told me."

Sébastien takes a shaky breath. Clearly, he's still suffering from the trauma. Perhaps because he's recently revisited it in the Boutique of Psychosis. "So, you and Dix?" His voice is not as firm as he'd like it to be.

"He came to me, asking for a favour."

"A favour?"

"When he saw me with Gaspar and heard how I spoke with other ghosts, the way I treated them as people not... tools, he wanted that for himself. He asked me to help him leave GoPol."

"And you agreed?" The hurt in his eyes is almost unbearable.

I bow my head and nod. "How could I not?"

Sébastien huffs softly. "Well, he got what he wanted then. I have no idea where he is, and he isn't responding to my calls." He's so clearly conflicted it hurts my heart.

"So, what's next?" I ask. "You don't want him gone and you've disobeyed your father. And now you're here. In my bedroom, returning my whisper ghost to me. What's the plan?" He must have one, otherwise, he wouldn't be here.

Sébastien swallows heavily, as if he still has to come to terms with his decision. "I want you to help me find Dix. Not to get him killed, but because..." Helplessly, he shrugs.

"You miss him?" It's so sad that he can't even express these feelings, just because his father taught him that ghosts were nothing but tools. "Dix once told me what frightened him most was that he felt replaceable. But he's not, right? You like him. He's a part of you, a reflection of you, and a constant reminder of what you've lost. But he's also your friend. Your *only* friend."

He suddenly looks up at me, hungry for more. "I thought..." His voice falters. Annoyed, he clears his throat. "I thought we might be friends as well."

I'd be lying if I said yes. Truth is I enjoy spending time with Sébastien. Sure, he's got a stick up his arse, but he's kind, thoughtful, and even a little funny. I remember how he came up with the ugly clown present for Hélène and Cédric. We definitely bonded over our difficulties with certain family members. But I was never truly able to trust him. I still don't know if I can now.

"Look..."

Quickly, Sébastien raises a hand. "Forget I said that." When I frown, he takes a deep breath. "As I said, I'm not stupid. I'm well aware that after everything that's happened to you, you have no reason to trust me. But I want you to know that, for the most part, I had your best interests at heart."

He was definitely fishing for my whisper ghost, and likely because it's in his job description, but I remember how he gave me space when we first met. How he recognised I had to come to terms with Gaspar's ghostliness. And even after we compared notes, he never actually went behind my back. That was all Cédric.

"You surprised me," Sébastien continues. "When I was growing up, I learnt all about ghosts. I'd never seen one, but I'd heard all the stories. My father told me how GoPol was working with them, and how much potential they bore. What he failed to mention was that I shouldn't forget they were once humans, too. I feel stupid now," he admits, "not seeing it for myself, even when I started working with them. It feels like I was blinkered, like I only saw part of the picture. The part I could take advantage of. And then you came into my life."

The way he's looking at me with his startling blue eyes makes me swallow. I'm becoming acutely aware again how scantily clad I am right now.

"You took the blinkers away, and for the first time, I saw clearly. I didn't want to believe it at first—just like you didn't trust your gut about me—but the proof was undeniable. When those ghosts came to our help in the Boutique... no one's ever done that for me."

The sad thing is that his "no one" doesn't just encompass ghosts, but literally *no one*.

"I want..." His voice breaks again, as if he's struggling to articulate what he really wants. "I would like to learn more. To understand more. What you just said about Dix... I feel horrible. He... he's irreplaceable to me." Sébastien is starting to blink more frequently, and once again, he's unable to meet my eyes. "Don't get me wrong. He annoys me a lot. He's not like the other whisper ghosts. Like C-Trente, who does *exactly* what my father says, even if that means sitting in his office for days and days on end. Contrary to that, Dix is constantly messing around and making horrible jokes, but I could always rely on him to be there. He's so much more than just a dead part of me. He's my friend. My brother. In a way, I guess." Awkwardly, Sébastien runs his hand across his neck and shrugs.

My heart warms a little. His feelings seem genuine, especially in regard to Dix, and I feel sorry for him that Dix's just ran off. Then again, Dix knows Sébastien better than anyone else. If he couldn't trust him, then neither should I. Not fully at least. I'd be stupid to after the debacle with Cédric.

"So, you and me," I say, then bite my tongue, unsure of what is *I* want.

Sébastien takes his hand off his neck and looks up at me. "I'll be honest, I don't have a complete plan. Obviously, we need to find Dix first, but then..." He takes a deep breath. "I think the work we do at GoPol is important. In theory, at least. No, I know it is. We've been able to avert at least four terror attacks in the last three years because of what we do, but I no longer agree with the methods. I think we could be even more effective if we did it your way."

"No one will ever do it my way at GoPol."

"Not as long as my father's in charge, that's for sure."

I suck in a breath. "What are you saying?"

He deflates a little again, struggling. "I don't know. I guess... I guess, we need to find a way to change things. To make it possible for people like you to continue existing, to foster positive relationships with the dead, and to stop... to stop this 'whatever means to an end' strategy my father is currently employing."

In the end, he can't say it. That he wants to stop his father from murdering him or others in the name of the mission. We still have a lot of work to do, but I promised Gaspar I'd fight. To not let GoPol be the end of me. And if that means partnering up with Sébastien, it's what I have to do.

"Alright. Let's trial this."

His eyes widen with surprise. "You're in?"

"To be clear, I want your father gone. Like, behind bars for the rest of his life. Because what he did to you and to the Chevalier and to me is unacceptable." Someone needs to say it.

Sébastien gulps, but he doesn't protest, which I take as a good sign.

"So, how do we do this? I've officially lost my ghost powers." Which means I need to be careful around ghosts. It's probably fine at the Panthéon where it's unlikely I'll be monitored, but I can't let slip in front of my family, either. Especially not in front of Hélène and Cédric. I'll have to continue grieving. Most importantly, though, I cannot under any circumstances acknowledge the presence of GoPol's whisper ghosts. "You need to teach me how to instantly recognise a ghost, so I don't accidentally start talking to them when I shouldn't."

"It isn't easy, but we can work on it."

"Good." Now, if we want to succeed, we'll have to see a lot more of each other. "How will you explain that you're still hanging out with me, even though I've lost all my powers and am the most horrible person who ever crossed your father's threshold? In case, you don't know, Cédric's the one who betrayed me. He'll most definitely betray you if he sees us together."

"Oh, for sure." I'm glad, Sébastien agrees with me there. Then again, there was never any love lost between the cousins. It makes me like him a little more. "Uhm, I thought I'd tell my father I'm keeping an eye on you. Your whisper ghost might be gone, but you still know a lot about the agency. There's no knowing what *harm* you could do."

That would definitely work for Charles, but only for Sébastien's part in it. "It wouldn't explain why *I* would let you be around me. The last thing your father knows is that I stole from him. Twice."

Sébastien's eyes widen. "Twice?"

I wave him off. We'll get to the Chevalier's file later. Maybe. "Why would I suddenly be cool with you?"

"Because we're friends?" he asks cautiously. "You feel you could trust me, even though you don't trust GoPol."

I'd have to be pretty naïve to do that. It needs to be something stronger. The solution is annoying—I don't want to do it—but I can see how it'd work for his father, for Cédric, and even for Hélène. "We start dating."

His eyes grow even bigger. "What?"

"Not immediately, of course. We need to be strategic. I don't trust you, but you've come to me to apologise." He hasn't actually done that yet. "I blow you off, but you keep making the effort. It's a ploy if your father asks, a way for you to keep tabs on me. And slowly, you'll win me over. Then we'll start hanging out. Not at GoPol or anything, but normal stuff. Date stuff."

Sébastien is all ears, which must mean my idea isn't as terrible as I'd thought.

"No one will question it. Hélène will be happy to see me moving on from my ghosts, while Cédric will pat his own shoulder, thinking he's done the right thing for me in the end. And then we'll get to work."

This is obviously a long-term commitment. We won't find Dix in a week, nor will we bring down GoPol in a month, but I need to lay low for a while to avoid suspicion and get Charles off my back. It'll also keep Sébastien safe from discovery.

He clears his throat. "Are you sure you want to do this?"

Gaspar comes to mind and my heart feels like it's being squashed by iron bands. Sébastien needs to find Dix, but I need to find Gaspar. Something I can't do if I'm being watched. Once I find him, I'll explain everything. Besides, it's not like I'm going to kiss Sébastien or anything. "Do you have a better idea?"

"No, it's pretty solid."

"Good, it's happening then. Time for you to go. Call me in two days."

"For?"

"To check in on me. Remember? You're trying to win me over?"

He cracks one of his rare smiles. "I've never done anything like this."

"I'll send you instructions." Clearly, he's overwhelmed by the idea of striking up a genuine connection with another person.

"Very well." He gets up, then glances at Petite Alix, who's still quietly playing with Malou. Malou must've sensed she's needed as a support animal right now, because she stays incredibly calm. "You'll have to find another safe space for her. GoPol can't see you with her."

"I've got something in mind." Surprisingly, I do. Victor said I should've brought her to the Panthéon from the beginning. Knowing how powerful the ghosts in there are, it seems like the obvious choice. The best thing is, no whisper ghosts will be able to spy on me there, since they're not letting anyone in. I'm not going to tell Sébastien, though, and I appreciate him not asking for clarification.

Instead, he crouches down in front of Petite Alix and awkwardly ruffles her hair. "Goodbye, little one." His gaze falls on Malou, and I remember our discussion about ghost-seeing hedgehogs. He's definitely got his proof now.

"You can touch her spikes," I encourage him.

Petite Alix is stroking Malou's back continuously, but she stops to let Sébastien have a go, looking at him with wide eyes. Slowly, he lowers his hand, cupping it as if he's afraid of hurting himself. Or maybe he's afraid of hurting Malou. His fingers brush across her, very lightly at first. As he tries again, he slowly gains confidence. And suddenly, there's a blissful little smile I've never seen on his lips before. Like a little boy and his first pet.

"I thought, she'd be spikier," he whispers.

13

Malou's found herself another fan.

After a few more strokes, he gets up, and nods at me. "I'll call you in two days." He's almost at the door before he turns. "And for what it's worth, I'm deeply sorry for everything."

CHAPTER 2

O nce Sébastien has left, I start getting dressed. It's as if the fog
of the last few days has finally lifted. I put my useless phone
on the charger and watch the blinking battery symbol. I'll have a
few minutes to myself before a deluge of messages and missed calls
come in, which I use to freshen up. Malou is content to keep Petite
Alix company and the little girl is so withdrawn, she's happy to sit
in the corner and not care about anything else.

"You look good," Maman comments when I leave the bathroom
in a more respectable state. "It was a good visit, then?"

I wouldn't exactly call Sébastien's visit good, but it definitely
woke me up. "There's a couple of things I need to take care of. I'll
probably be late."

Maman frowns. "Okay, but call, alright?"

"Sure will." I give her a quick kiss and hug that surprises her
before returning to my room.

With the door behind me, I think of Gaspar. It's not like he hasn't been on my mind, though I can't remember if I've actually tried to call him. He's always appeared before, but even when I speak his name, the room remains empty.

My eyes fill with tears and there's a familiar pain in my chest. I squeeze my eyes shut and shove the matter of Gaspar to the side for now. There are other things to do.

I grab my phone, now filled with notifications. Thirty-two missed calls from Gaby alone and dozens of messages, some worried, some mildly threatening. It's a wonder she hasn't waltzed into my room yet. But she's not the only one who's texted. Sébastien's called and there's hundreds of messages in the class chat. Everyone's been working on their assignments. I have exactly one day to catch up. Fun times.

And then there's an eight-message thread from Hélène, starting with *"You need help, Alix. Proper…"*

Instead of opening the thread, I delete the messages. No one needs that kind of negativity right now. And as for help; I'm not the one marrying a psychopath.

I type a quick message to Gaby that I'm fine and I'll visit later tonight, but there's something more pressing I need to take care of. I'm instantly inundated with messages.

OMG, Alix!

You're alive.

???

What does that mean?

Can I just call you?

I smile as her worry washes over my screen. *I'll be by LATER. Promise.* I add a love heart emoji, which is a pale representation of how much I love her.

Okay. I'll get some wine. Bisous.

We'll definitely need wine.

I leave the phone to charge up a bit more and turn to Petite Alix. "Hey, sweetie. It's time for us to go. Shall we put Malou back and—"

The little girl quickly shakes her head and holds Malou closer to her chest.

"Okay. We can take her with us. Look, she's got a little leash and a special place in my bag." I gather the items and show Petite Alix how to fit the leash. Malou raises her nose, getting a bit more active and ready to run. I give the end to Alix so she feels included and gently pull her to her feet.

Then I put some food for Malou into the bag, grab my phone and the charger, and get ready to leave.

It's snowing outside, so Petite Alix and I take the Métro. I let her hold the leash while Malou sits in her bag, shielded from the outside world, and otherwise try to ignore her presence. I usually

17

do my best to avoid interacting with ghosts so I don't get funny looks from strangers, but this time it's different. It's absolutely vital for my safety—and that of the little girl next to me—that no one sees me interacting with people who aren't visible to everyone else. If even a rumour of this gets back to GoPol, I'll lose my ability for real.

I don't know if it's real or just paranoia, but I feel watched all the way to the Panthéon. Several people get out with me at the stop and I leave Petite Alix to totter along on Malou's lead as I make my way to the upper world, the hairs on the back of my neck standing up.

There's still a man and a woman following me from the Métro. The man's studying his phone, seemingly in his own world, while the woman holds back. Too slow. She's middle-aged and dressed for business. She's the type who usually strides past me because their time is too precious to waste strolling. If only Sébastien had taught me to spot ghosts at a glance already.

I decide to play it safe and glance past, as if I don't see them, as I continue on my way. The man eventually takes another path, but the woman continues to follow me. Maybe it's all in my head, but there's no way I can take Petite Alix to the Panthéon with a potential GoPol spy on my tail. The last thing I want is to bring despair and destruction upon my dear friends.

Just as I'm about to turn left instead of right into the square, the woman turns on her heel and walks the other way, as leisurely as before. I stay, curious to see if she'll turn back, but she keeps on walking, not even looking over her shoulder.

I feel my heart pounding as I decide to cross the square after all. There's no one waiting for me under the columns or any other dubious figures in the square, so Petite Alix and I manage to enter without being stopped. Inside, Philippe is about to close up. I dodge his surprised question by telling him I forgot something in the crypt, and hurry past before I get wrapped up in small talk.

Part of me is worried I've lost my ability to see ghosts. Sure, Petite Alix is here by my side, but Gaspar isn't. Before the thought gets out of hand, three of Napoleon's generals salute and greet me. "Good evening, Mademoiselle Alix."

I almost burst into tears of relief. I manage to walk on and stumble down the stairs to the crypt. But when I see Victor standing there, all I can do is fall into his arms and sob. To others, he may be Victor Hugo, revered writer and politician. To me, he's become something of a surrogate father and dear friend.

"There you are," he says, with infinite warmth, stroking my hair. "We've been waiting for you to come back."

"You made it out alive, kid," a voice says from the bench on the other side. I look up and see Jean Moulin, heroic leader of the Résistance. He's usually styled impeccably, a high-collared coat, a red scarf, and a chic fedora, but he's sitting there in a torn shirt, his scarred neck exposed, hair dishevelled, a hint of bruising under his translucent skin. There are salt bullet holes in freaking Jean *Moulin*.

"What have they done to you?" I whisper.

Jean waves me away. "Nothing that won't heal in time. I got off lightly. Unlike you."

Thanks to Sébastien, I've never experienced any undue violence from the GoPol agents, and the modern police wouldn't dare abuse anyone in prison. Fortunately, that's mostly in the past. "I'm fine."

He stares at me. Finally he gives me a sharp nod. "Far from it, but I will honour your defiant spirit."

"You were followed," Jean Lannes, a Napoleon general, informs me. He salutes in front of Victor as if we were in the middle of war. "We turned the enemy away."

"So, she *was* a spy." I'm glad I'm not paranoid after all. "Was it a ghost?"

Lannes shakes his head. "No, this one was alive. But we've had several ghosts and humans snooping around."

"And you sent them away?" I try to understand what that means as I sit down next to Moulin, lifting Petite Alix onto my lap.

All the ghosts gather around, just as they did when we planned the infiltration of GoPol just a week ago. Josephine Baker squeezes my shoulder and Victor Hugo never truly leaves my side.

Lannes nods. "We did. You're safe here."

"But how?" I understand that they can keep ghosts out of the crypt, but what do they do to people?

Voltaire provides the answer. "This is a place of power, Mademoiselle Alix. It extends far beyond the realm of death. Any agent of the so-called ghost police, or anyone who wishes us or you ill, will find themselves very interested in other pressing matters."

The woman turning on her heel comes to mind. People seldom turn on the spot without at least looking lost. The idea that the Pántheon itself might have repelled her makes me feel queasy, and yet I can't help but breathe a sigh of relief. "This place is safe."

Victor's hand squeezes my shoulder. "You're safe here."

I take a deep breath, shaking at first, but then slowly calming down. Two tears run down my cheeks. Annoyed, I wipe them away. There's still more to do and this could very well turn into an argument. "Will it be safe for Petite Alix?" They've let her in, but my spirits are notoriously strict about protecting their sacred space.

"Of course she'll be safe here," Victor says. "You should have brought her to me in the first place."

"But you don't accept ghosts who aren't buried here."

Voltaire stiffens in front of me. "We do now."

Not that I want to argue with a good thing, but... "Why? What changed?"

"You have to ask?" Victor looks at me warmly. "You did. You changed us."

CHAPTER 3

Gaby greets me with a stern, "I was going to break down your door." She pulls me inside, hands me an over-full glass of red wine, and sits me on her bed. "I want to know everything."

Halfway through my story, I'm reduced to a puddle of tears. Gaby hugs me and coaxes the last details out until I've told her everything. The bad, the ugly, and the absolutely soul-shattering devastation. "And I still have my powers, but he's gone. Gaspar's gone."

"How could that be?"

I have a theory, and it makes my stomach churn so badly I almost throw up on Gaby's carpet. "What if he went back to GoPol?"

Her eyes widen? "To steal her again?"

He wouldn't have been able to. "Or to bargain with them." The only living who can see him are ghost whisperers, like me. "He could've pleaded my case, begged them to let me keep my powers, and then... and then..." I hiccup. "Then they shot him full of salt and dissolved every memory of him." There aren't enough tears to fill the hole Gaspar's disappearance has left.

Gaby hugs me tightly and rubs my shoulders until I can breathe a little. "Now, now, let's not get ahead of ourselves. There's no reason to assume he did something so reckless."

I'm not convinced. Gaspar was as heartbroken as I was, and I did something pretty reckless to escape from GoPol. "He's gone." I want to say *forever*, but I can't bring myself to say it out loud.

"No, he's not." Gaby shakes her head defiantly. "Maybe they took him prisoner, a bargaining chip to ensure your silence."

I want to ask how that's better, while fighting the urge to march down to GoPol on the spot. Instead, I force myself to reason. "But they never negotiated with me."

"They sent Sébastien." It was clear from the moment I told her that Gaby doesn't trust him at all.

Neither do I. Not really. "He didn't negotiate, either. Not like that."

"It could be a trap."

"Sure, but... they don't need a trap. If they want to silence me, there are much easier ways." It's a hard pill to swallow, but I have no power in this fight. I can't go to the police because they're intertwined. I'm not saying that every policeman is as corrupt as Officer Cédric, but GoPol is a government agency. They're protected. And as for any public avenues, I'm fresh out of hard evidence after Cédric stole the Chevalier's file.

In the meantime, they have the power to manipulate any evidence. There's probably some video camera footage that shows me breaking and entering. My fingerprints are all over GoPol and they've got all sorts of intimate knowledge about me. I've also signed what's effectively an NDA. There's no need for a trap, no need for negotiation. "My back's already against the wall."

Gaby sighs heavily. "I hate to see you like this. I wish you could just stop."

"Stop?"

"Stop being involved in all this." She raises her hand before I can protest. "I know! You're in too deep. That's why I said I wish you *could*."

I calm down and nod carefully. It would be so nice to go back to my old life of history lessons and ghost visits, but Gaby's right. I'm still on GoPol's radar, still a person of interest. They've got me under their thumb for now, but if they find out I can still see ghosts... they might just go for a more permanent solution.

"You can't tell anyone."

"What?"

"That I still have my powers. Not Odile, not Marie, no one. You and Sébastien are the only ones who know I haven't lost them." No one else can know.

Gaby looks a little tortured, probably because of Marie, but finally she nods. "I won't say a word. But I don't like the idea of Sébastien knowing."

"Well, it can't be helped," I say with a shrug. "He's the reason I still have them."

"I understand and I'm grateful, don't get me wrong. I also understand he wasn't the one who ratted you out or betrayed you, but... and this is a big one, he's so deeply rooted in everything GoPol stands for. He's the director's son, for goodness' sake!" Gaby claws at her own head, as if she just blew her own mind. "Do you really think he'll stand up for you when it counts? Or will he just run back to Daddy?"

That's a very good point. Sébastien's relationship with his father is complicated. The man murdered him, and yet Sébastien works for him. He was at Père Lachaise when GoPol cracked down on the ghosts there, and he was part of the raid in the catacombs. Maybe he just wanted to make sure I'd be safe, but that could be as much wishful thinking as anything else.

"Do you really need him?" Gaby asks.

What an interesting question. Sébastien came to me for help. We never talked about him doing something for me in return. On the other hand, he's already done something by bringing Petite Alix back. "Without him, I would've lost my ability."

Gaby's shoulders sag. "True. I'm just worried he'll get you into an even bigger mess with this search for his whisper ghost. I mean, his father is willing to kill him—again. What's to stop him from killing *you*?"

The scary answer is: not much. "I don't want to just roll over and die. Charles Roubert could decide to kill me any time. He's already having me followed. As it is, I've got two options: I can lay low, avoid any contact with the ghosts outside the Panthéon, and hope he'll eventually give up on me. Or I can do something about it." The second option flows much easier from my mouth.

"You've spent too much time with the ghosts of the Revolution," Gaby says, clicking her tongue. "And you're unable to say no when someone comes to you for help. It's just like one of your favours. Only this time the person's still alive."

"'Still' being the keyword here."

She slaps me for my insensitive joke. "But do you have to pretend to go out with him?"

"I think it's the best way to disguise what we're really doing. His father will think he's just keeping an eye on me, while Hélène will be happy I'm dating someone corporal."

"He's got that going for him," Gaby agrees.

This time it's my turn to bat at her. "I'm not going to cheat on Gaspar."

"I didn't say that." Gaby giggles. "Look, if that's what you want to do, I'm on your side. To be honest, I want nothing more than to kick GoPol's ass. I'm just not convinced by your choice of allies."

Neither am I. "Well, first we'll find Dix." And Gaspar. While Sébastien's allegiance is still unclear, his whisper ghost has taken a stand. If not for Sébastien's sake, I owe it to Dix to make sure he's safe. "Nobody's talking about overthrowing GoPol tomorrow."

"God, no!" Gaby shudders. Then she refills our glasses and raises them in a toast. "To new beginnings."

"To new beginnings."

CHAPTER 4

O ver the next few weeks I learn to be patient. At first, I was calling Gaspar several times a day, but never got an answer. I also tried calling Dix, who ignored me as much as he did Sébastien. Speaking of the latter, he's been following my instructions admirably. I've received flowers, chocolates, and, because Gaby really wanted to test his commitment, a bottle of genuine champagne. He's stuck to my carefully crafted script and we're now past the reconciliation period, ready to start with the "new relationship" phase.

So far it's all gone well. I've noticed that I no longer have a GoPol spy watching my every step outside, which means the news that Sébastien's on my case must have reached them. On the other hand, there's not much to report. GoPol is doing business as usual, ferreting out threats to the country, averting terror attacks, and sweeping up newly created whisper ghosts. Meanwhile, Sébastien's new whisper ghost creation is on hold until they find Dix. Not because his father cares, but because Sébastien has at least that much agency over his own life.

In the meantime, I've been busy with university stuff. Losing the whole Christmas break to rebellion and heartbreak has put me at a disadvantage, and exams are fast approaching. With Gaby's help I've managed to finish my homework, but as soon as I get home I'm either buried in my books, making flashcards, or giving Malou long lectures on my subjects.

Still, I feel woefully underprepared when I sit my first exam of the term. Gaby assures me I've studied enough and I only feel this way because my mind is elsewhere. In the end, she's right. As soon as I sit down and turn over the exam paper, my hand won't stop writing.

It's for the Parisian History class, and Madame Canet must love me or something, because more than half the questions and the little essay at the end are about the catacombs. By now I'm a bit of an expert, and I breeze through, even managing to finish early.

After a final rereading of my answers, I hand in my work and head for the fountain outside. It's a surprisingly beautiful February day, cold but sunny, giving the illusion of an early spring. I know better than to hope, but I still enjoy the sun on my face.

"That was a good one, wasn't it?"

Startled, I find Théo, my eternal adversary in class, taking a seat just a metre away from me. He smiles. "You handed in early, so I assume you found it just as easy as I did."

"What makes you think I didn't just give up?"

Théo cocks his head and laughs. "You? Giving up? That's not the Alix I know. If you'd been struggling with this exam, you'd have spent every damn last minute scrambling for points."

I want to tell him he doesn't know me, but unfortunately that does sound a lot like me. "Yeah, it was okay."

There's an awkward silence. I haven't been alone with Théo since... well, never really. I usually have Gaby acting as a buffer, and he has his own posse who don't want anything to do with the class weirdo. But they're all still in the examination room.

"Have you done the final report on Methods?" Théo asks out of the blue.

Or maybe it's not so out of the blue. After all, it's just what you'd expect from a classmate. The problem is, firstly, my life is so far from normal that normal's started to feel strange, and secondly, Théo's never treated me normally before.

"Almost," I answer, considering whether or not to confront him about his behaviour. God knows the last thing I need is more drama in my life.

Théo opens his mouth again before being distracted by the sound of a motorbike. We both watch as the rider banks the bike and effortlessly parks it right next to us. As he takes off his helmet and shakes out his short blond hair, I can't help but smile.

Just what I needed.

I jump up from the edge of the fountain. "That's my ride." Sébastien is early. Perfect.

"That's..." Théo seems lost for words. "Um, is he...?"

"That's my boyfriend, yes." I go over and kiss Sébastien's cheeks. He hands me his spare helmet, barely acknowledging Théo. "How was the exam?"

"Really good. I think I aced it."

I've never ridden a motorbike before, but in front of Théo I put the helmet on as if it's second nature to me and climb behind Sébastien without hesitation.

"Ready to go?"

I nod and together we pull away from the kerb, leaving Théo in the dust.

For our first official date, Sébastien drives us to Montmartre. When I see the white domes of the Basilica Sacré-Cœur rising above the rooftops, I feel a strange flutter in my stomach. Going to beautiful places like this almost feels like I'm on a real date. Only the man I've got my arms around isn't the one I'm desperate to hold.

Suddenly I'm nervous about the whole plan. How far do we have to go with this charade? I don't think I could handle a real date, even if it's something as innocuous as visiting the basilica, sitting on the steps, and gazing at the city below. Gaspar and I never had the chance to do something like that, a normal date, and it feels wrong to have one with Sébastien first.

But then Sébastien drives past the tourist car park and around the corner to park somewhere less romantic, and I can't help but smile again.

"The cemetery?" I ask as I get off the bike and take off my helmet. "Very romantic."

Sébastien looks at me alarmed. "Did I get it wrong? Did you—?"

I laugh at him. "No, no. This is perfect. Fitting. For us." Where else would you find two ghost whisperers?

He smiles shyly. "I thought we could combine this date with our first lesson." He stows the helmets away and offers me his arm. "Shall we?"

"First lesson?" Cautiously I take his arm.

He leans in and lowers his voice. "How to tell the dead from the living."

I take a sharp breath, then nod. "Let's do it." Before I got involved with GoPol and the Résistance, knowing would've saved me from a few embarrassing moments here and there. Now, it's literally a matter of life and death.

The Cimetière de Montmartre is smaller than Père Lachaise and Montparnasse. Only about 20,000 people are buried here. Most of it's flat with neat rows of tombstones, statues, and family crypts. All kinds of trees have been planted between the graves, enough that I can imagine the shade their leaves would provide in the summer.

Although it's a warm day, it's not exactly tourist season. And while Montmartre has its share of famous people like Degas and Ampère, it doesn't have the draw of the larger cemeteries. If I had to guess, I'd say about two-thirds of the people I see are dead.

"Obvious things first," says Sébastien.

"Period dress. Open wounds." Two men in 19th-century garb are debating the Prussian threat to our left, while a woman with a slit throat strolls past us.

Sébastien nods darkly. "Don't look."

Immediately, my heart's in my throat. "Is someone following us?"

"No, but as soon as you look at a ghost, you're giving yourself away."

I groan. "How am I supposed to decide if someone is alive or dead without looking at them?"

"Peripheral vision. Avoid looking people in the eye." Sébastien turns to me with a distant look, as if there's something more interesting at the back of the cemetery. "I often look past the ear to find something that catches the eye. A poster, a Métro clock or, in this case, an interesting statue. Then you move your eyes across the face to look at something else".

As he demonstrates, looking eerily as if he can't see me, I feel my anxiety rise. "And in that quick movement, you identify them?"

Sébastien's lips curl into a mischievous grin. "I've already noticed all I need to know by looking past them. This last glance is just for confirmation."

As easy as he makes it sound, I still have so many questions. "So, what are you looking for?"

"Little things. We've already covered clothing and wounds. One of the easiest tells is bad weather."

"Bad weather?"

"Ghosts aren't affected by the weather like we are. Someone's skin is completely dry in the pouring rain? Ghost. Their hair doesn't move at all when the wind blows through it? Ghost again." Sébastien smiles. "You know this."

I remember Dix crawling through the catacombs in T-shirt and trainers, both as clean as if they'd just come out of the washing machine. "Gaspar got wet," I say. At least I don't remember him staying dry after he carried me through the Banga.

Sébastien nods thoughtfully. "Gaspar is too young. As a ghost, I mean. His soul still remembers water is wet. The older ghosts... well, they forget they should get wet. Just like they forget it's not normal to walk around with a bullet wound." He pulls a face when a ghost with a ruined face passes us.

"Why are they doing this anyway?" I ask, watching the ghost over my shoulder. "Holding onto their death like that?" In my mind, I see Jean Moulin writhing on the ground with terrible wounds.

"Why are you still afraid of drowning?" I give him a long stare and Sébastien shrugs. "I don't know, but I imagine it has something to do with the effect death has on a person. Wouldn't you agree it's quite dramatic?"

I notice he's rubbing his left wrist with his thumb. Is he remembering his own death now? Since I found out what his father did to him, I've avoided thinking about it. "How did he do it?" I whisper, nodding gently towards his wrist.

Caught red-handed, Sébastien pulls down his jacket. "Electric shock."

I wish I hadn't asked, because now I see Sébastien strapped to a table while his father administers the fatal shock. Just before he brings him back. That's why Sébastien couldn't move in the Boutique of Psychosis.

"Well, when all else fails," Sébastien says, clearing his throat, "when they have no obvious clues in their appearance or behaviour, there's something we call 'the ghost pull'."

"'The ghost pull'?" I look at him curiously. "What's that?"

"It describes an effect that's only been observed in ghost whisperers. It's an innate feeling deep in your gut, a pull that draws you

35

to a ghost. And the ghost to you. Haven't you ever noticed how they seek you out?"

"That's because they know me. I mean, ghosts talk to each other. Many know me and my reputation."

He regards me with curiosity. "Your reputation to help them?" When I nod, he frowns unhappily. "That could be a problem."

"Isn't that why we're here? To make it not my problem anymore?"

Sébastien's jaw moves as he thinks. "If you're no longer a ghost whisperer, the ghosts shouldn't seek you out."

I groan softly as the realisation hits me. "So even if I recognise them instantly, the fact they come to me could give me away?"

He nods sharply. "For a while, we could get away with the excuse that the spirits don't know you've stopped seeing them. But you can't acknowledge them. At all. For your own safety, you have to assume everyone's a ghost."

"Until proven alive." I groan. At the moment, the task seems insurmountable. I've never been much of an actor, yet somehow I've landed the role of a lifetime. Dread fills me and I feel like giving up.

Just then, Sébastien's fingers caress my hand. "Don't despair yet. I'll teach you and you'll be up to speed in no time. Maybe you can tell your ghost friends to spread the word, make sure everyone backs off a bit." He almost holds my hand. "Gaspar could run interference." His fingers fall away immediately. "Where is he, by the way? Is he staying away from this," Sébastien swallows, "date?"

I fight back a wave of sadness and smile. "Something like that."

He doesn't even question me. Somehow Sébastien trusts me like no one else or he believes pushing me won't get him anywhere. "This isn't forever, Alix."

"What is?"

"You having to hide what you are."

I snort and walk on. "I've always had to hide what I am. Now, instead of being ridiculed, I'll get killed for it."

"Not on my watch."

His low growl makes me stop and glance back at him. There's no amusement in his face, just simple, serious determination. It makes me uncomfortable, as if I should react somehow, but no one's taught me how. "Let's practice, shall we?" I owe it to him to at least try.

Sébastien nods and closes the distance between us. I take his arm to make us look like a couple taking a stroll along the cemetery paths. Without ever looking at the other people, I rely on my gut feeling when he asks.

"The woman on the bench."

"Dead.'"

"The caretaker with the rake."

"Dead."

"The old woman at the grave."

"Alive. But her husband isn't."

Now that I'm concentrating on each person, it's quite easy. Sébastien chooses difficult people, the ones who could very well be alive, and each time I try to listen to a voice inside me. I don't know if I can feel this pull he spoke of, but every time I concentrate on something, my instinct puts a verdict on my lips. At first I don't trust it, searching instead for clues to confirm my suspicions, but it's rarely wrong and slowly my answers come faster.

"See, it's not that difficult."

"It's easy here, because of the necropolis. Almost everyone is dead."

Sébastien cocks his head. "That's why I brought you here. It's a start. You expect almost everyone to be dead. It'll be harder to spot the ghost if you expect everyone to be alive."

I think back to the first time I met Gaspar. Although I'd stopped at the scene of his accident, I didn't know anyone had died. So many people had gathered I'd assumed everyone around me was alive. But he was drawn to me. Because I'm a ghost whisperer.

And then I just forgot to question it. Just like ghosts forget to get wet when it rains.

As the first drops of rain fall, cutting short our walk, I turn to Sébastien. "He's gone."

"Who is?"

My breath shakes. "Gaspar."

Sébastien's face immediately darkens with worry. "How? Where did he go? Was he salted?"

The last question hits a little too close to home and I gasp. "I hope not. I mean, I don't know." *Deep breaths, Alix. Deep breaths.* "He came out of the sting operation just fine. We held each other the night after and said goodbye in case I..." This is too hard. "The next morning he was gone. And no matter how much I call him..." My eyes fill with tears. "Sorry, I... he's gone."

"Like Dix."

"Like Dix." Only Dix has gone rogue and Gaspar is no whisper ghost. I swallow my tears, trying to shut down the emotions. "I thought maybe he tried to negotiate with GoPol."

"I haven't seen or heard from him."

It's not a hundred per cent security—Sébastien may not be privy to everything that goes on at GoPol—but it's enough to keep my hope alive. "Maybe they're together." Maybe he contacted Dix and the two of them are working on some secret plan.

Sébastien gives me a cautious smile. "Maybe." Then he swallows, clearly not really entertaining the possibility. "I'll keep an eye out."

A few stupid tears still find their way down my cheek. "Thank you."

"Let's get you home."

Spotting dead people and crying over another guy. It's safe to say our first date went splendidly.

CHAPTER 5

B y the time Sébastien drops me off at home, the beautiful day has turned sour, and the slight drizzle has turned into a downpour. The sky has darkened and the light from the lanterns is reflected in the mirrored glaze of the cobbled streets.

"Drive carefully," I say, as I give him back his helmet and take off the leather jacket he's lent me. It's too late to save his jumper, but it's the thought that counts. I lean over and kiss him on the cheek, in case anyone is watching from the window. "I'll text you with the next steps."

He nods at me. "Keep practising."

"Will do." I hurry to the door, taking cover under the short awning while I get my key out. It's only when I'm in the hallway that I realise Sébastien is still there, watching me.

I give him a small smile and wave before letting the door close behind me. Despite the wet end to our date, I was having a surprisingly good time. None of it was romantic—which was kind of the point—but we built a connection, however fragile it may be. When I look at Sébastien, I see my loneliness, the knowledge of having no one who shares our experience of this strange existence between life and death.

And we both have problems with our dear relatives, I muse when I notice my sister's fancy shoes next to Cédric's sturdy boots in the corridor. The sight of their shoes alone is enough for me to write off the rest of the day. I've been avoiding Hélène since she threw me out of her car on New Year's Day, and I certainly don't want to cross her fiancé's path after he betrayed me to his uncle.

I ignore the laughter in the living room and slip into my room, closing the door carefully, just as someone behind me clears their throat.

"Bonsoir, Mademoiselle Dubois."

I almost let out a scream, but manage to hold it in. There's a man—or rather a ghost—in my room. This one's easy to spot as his fancy dress has been out of fashion for at least a hundred and fifty years. It's not someone I recognise. What makes matters worse is I suddenly hear Cédric's voice in the corridor.

"...Thursday morning. Let me just get my wallet."

My future brother-in-law is now on the other side of the door, rummaging through his coat. I stare at the ghost and put my finger to my lips, praying to anyone who hears me I don't do anything stupid and give myself away. Like talking to myself in my own room.

Cédric takes his sweet time getting his wallet, which makes me extra grumpy. It's not like he has a huge handbag to rummage through.

"Oh, looks like Alix came home," he calls out, making me want to wring his neck.

"I just..." the ghost in front of me starts, but I cut him off with a rude finger across my neck.

There's the dreaded knock. "Alix?" Cédric asks. "Come, join us in the living room. We're celebrating my promotion."

Is he really that tone-deaf or does he take some perverse pleasure in rubbing it in? I consider pretending I'm not in my room, but *Officer* Cédric has already deduced my presence from my wet boots.

"I'd rather drown myself," I say instead, my voice full of acid.

There's a heavy sigh on the other side of the door. "Can we talk?" And before I can answer, the doorknob turns.

I turn the lock just in time before he can violate the privacy of my room. The thing is, I don't know how much he's been promoted. Has he already joined the ranks of ghost whisperers? If so, seeing a ghost in my room is just the proof he needs to ruin me completely.

"Can we not?" I shoot back through the door. "Seriously. Leave me alone."

"Alix, please. I just want to explain."

"You can shove that explanation up your ass. If there's any room left," I add sourly.

The insult seem to confuse him, because he takes a long time to answer. When he does, it's just a simple, "Um, okay." Another sigh. "Well, if you change your mind, my door's always open."

How infuriating can a person be? I can't believe he's still playing the concerned, caring older brother card, when he's the one who betrayed me for his own advancement. Then it hits me. He's still not satisfied. There's still more to gain by using me. Like proving I'm still a ghost whisperer.

Fortunately, he's given up for now. His footsteps fade and I wait until I hear his muffled voice in the living room. Then I rush over to the ghost and whisper, "You can't be here. What do you want?"

If the ghost thinks my behaviour is unseemly, he doesn't show it. "I have a message for you. From him."

"Him?"

The ghost looks at me confusedly, as if it's only now occurred to him that "him" isn't much of an identifier. But instead of clarifying, he simply says, "He wishes for you to attend the performance of Médée at the opera this Saturday. Your invitation has already been delivered by mortal means. I'm here to emphasise the importance of your visit."

"Why?" I bite my lip to stop myself from asking a more detailed question when I hear footsteps in the corridor again.

"He didn't say. Just that he wishes to see you." Again, the ghost seems confused by the lack of information. "To be honest, he's a bit... spooky."

A ghost calling another one spooky is certainly a first. I don't know what to make of the ominous invitation. It sounds like another favour. If so, I'm out of business. Unfortunately, I can't tell the ghost that, because my sister is knocking on the door now.

"Alix?" Hélène sounds annoyed. "Could you please stop moping and come out and talk like an adult?"

Exactly the kind of words to make you feel loved and supported. I roll my eyes at the ghost in a show of empathy, but he's already gone. Well, at least that's one less threat to deal with.

"You're being ridiculous. We've got something to celebrate today. With the *whole* family. So would you please open the door and join us?"

I do her the favour, but not for the reason she proposes. "I'm not his family," I tell her to her face, and push past her.

My feet actually lead me into the living room, where my whole family is sitting around the table to enjoy what looks like a fancy dinner and champagne. My mother lights up when she sees me. "Alix. Come join us. Cédric has some fabulous news to share."

Next to her, my younger sister Odile rolls her eyes, echoing my feelings about our future brother-in-law.

"Trust me, I know all about it." I smile sweetly at Cédric. "I should get a share of your pay rise." And compensation for the damage done to me. "Where's the mail?" I ask Papa.

He and Maman exchange a confused look prompted by my absurd demand. Then he points to a flat glass bowl on the dresser. "There's a letter for you. Fancy looking."

I fish it out of the bowl, admiring the thick paper envelope and the ornate handwriting. It looks like something from another century too.

"Who's it from?" asks Hélène, who's followed me into the room.

There's no return address on the envelope. I ignore my sister and open it. Inside are two tickets and a short note:

Dear Alix,

Please join me for a spectacular night at the opera.

Yours sincerely.

There's no signature here, either. Apparently, I'm supposed to guess who my mysterious benefactor is. For a moment I hope it's Gaspar, but he can't send letters, let alone buy tickets for the opera. And by the looks of it, they're expensive private box tickets.

"Don't keep us on the rack for so long," says Maman, amused. "What is it?"

I snap out of my reverie, knowing I have to think on my feet. Whoever sent me this is someone connected to the ghost world. It could be an elaborate trap, or it could be the Chevalier reaching out to me... or it could be some powerful ghost I haven't met yet. The fact is none of these possibilities are meant for Hélène's or Cédric's ears.

Instead, I decide to go ahead with my previous plan. "They're opera tickets from my boyfriend. Nothing special."

Maman gasps with delight. "Nothing special? Alix, I didn't even know you had a boyfriend. Is he the one who sent you flowers last week?"

Hélène narrows her eyes, probably thinking of Gaspar, who I shouldn't be able to see anymore.

Before she can ask any incriminating questions, I smile at my mother. "Yes. It's all quite new."

"Are we going to meet him?" Maman asks excitedly.

I'm well aware of Cédric's gaze, although I look past him, just as Sébastien taught me. "If it goes well." It hurts to say the words. I couldn't introduce her to Gaspar, but Sébastien presents no such problem. "Anyway. I have to study, so I'll eat later." When Hélène and Cédric have left.

Before anyone can protest, I push past Hélène and return to my room. Just as I'm about to close the door, Odile slips in.

"Are they from Gaspar?" she whispers as soon as the door is closed.

"Not that I know of. Remember, I can no longer talk to him. Or see him." I give her a dejected, one-sided shrug.

Odile has been a wonderful sister to me lately, much better than Hélène. She's taken my side in the conflict with GoPol and fully supported my relationship with Gaspar, even though she can't see him. She's also been incredibly brave, risking the wrath of GoPol.

And that's why she can't know I'm still a ghost whisperer. I can't involve her again.

She looks at me sympathetically before suddenly frowning. "So, who's the boyfriend?"

I wish I could blush at her question, but that's way beyond my meagre acting skills. All I can do is lower my eyes and whisper the name of my fake boyfriend. "Sébastien."

Odile's eyes widen. "Sébas... Alix, I thought he betray—"

"Ssh!" I look at the door in panic. Has Cédric snuck out again to listen in? "He's not who I thought he was. He apologised. It was all a misunderstanding, you know?" Judging by Odile's heavy frown, I'm not really selling this relationship to her. "We've been on a date or two. Like I said, it's very new."

"Can you trust him?"

"More than his cousin and his fiancée."

"You mean our sister?" Odile calls me out.

"She's no sister of mine." It's a bit harsh, but Hélène made her choice when she threw in her lot with Cédric and refused to listen to a single word I said. "Anyway, it's time for me to live in the world of the living, isn't it?" I look at the letter, which is neither from Gaspar *nor* Sébastien. "This is a good thing."

Odile's frown melts into an expression of sympathy. I must have moved her, because she opens her arms and pulls me into a comforting embrace. "Everything will be fine."

If only.

CHAPTER 6

After telling my family the ominous tickets were from Sébastien, I decide I should also inform him about his unexpected gift. The next day, before our "Period of Enlightenment" exam, Gaby and I claim a table at *Chambelland* and quickly cover the surface with flash cards and coffee cups.

While I wait for Sébastien, we use the time to study. Marie serves a few customers before refilling our cups and handing me a pain au chocolat.

"I didn't order one."

"It's on the house." Marie smiles as she sits on Gaby's lap. "I'm so sorry about Gaspar."

Gaby's kept her word and hasn't told anyone about my intact powers, not even her girlfriend, although I can see it's killing her to keep it secret.

I don't like it much more, either. Like Odile, Marie jumped in to help me, even enlisting her Knight Hospitaller uncle to help me escape. For a moment I was worried I'd got them into trouble, but no one saw them. To keep it that way, I must keep up my act. "It's alright. We were never meant to be, anyway."

Marie looks at me sadly. "I know it's silly, but it's as if he's died a second time. I can't even feel his presence in the shop anymore."

I don't know why this hits me so hard. Of course Marie can't feel him either. It's not like he's hiding from me. Gaspar is just gone. *Died a second time*, as Marie put it so aptly.

Gaby reaches across the table. It's only when she rubs my hand that I notice the tears in my eyes. I blink quickly and dig into the pain au chocolat to eat my emotions, only to remember how it was Gaspar who brought me here in the first place.

"If there's anything I can do, just let me know. Anything," Marie says with the kind of honesty that goes straight to the heart. I know why Gaby's absolutely smitten with her. Marie glances around the shop, as if worried someone's snuck in. "I know it's exam time, but what are we going to do about it?"

"About what?"

Even though we're still alone, Marie lowers her voice. "About GoPol and everything they do. Someone has to expose them."

Below her, Gaby squirms uncomfortably. She gives me a sharp look and I know exactly what she means. We should trust Marie. But they've only been together for two months, and Marie is as new to this as my little sister. Her uncle could be a valuable ally—*if* the Maltesers were opposed to GoPol. From what I know of his attitude towards ghosts, I doubt he'd take my side. He'd probably say it was a blessing. That I no longer have to worry about the wishes of the dead.

"I appreciate it, I really do, but I'd rather just put it behind me."

Marie's eyes widen. Her voice is full of passion as she continues. "But what they're doing is wrong. On so many accounts." Not sure GoPol would agree there. "I'm sorry, I understand they scared you, but it's not just you, is it? You're not the first person to have your powers taken away, and you won't be the last." She looks at Gaby. "We have to do something."

"It's dangerous," Gaby says quietly, shooting me another long look.

"A lot of things are dangerous. Joining the Résistance was dangerous. Every single revolution has been dangerous. But they *mattered*. You have to fight for what's right."

"Have I ever told you how beautiful you are when you're passionate about something?" Gaby deflects expertly. She means it, too, judging by the lovelorn look she gives Marie.

Marie immediately blushes and laughs. She loses some of the tension and sighs. "I'm not saying we should start a revolution, but we can't let them get away—"

She stops when the doorbell rings, announcing a new customer. It's Sébastien. He's soon followed by two female students who regard him with great interest.

"I have to go," Marie says, "but we'll talk later."

Sébastien passes her on his way and greets first Gaby, then me, before pulling up a chair to sit right next to me. "Sorry I'm late." As he puts his arm around my shoulders, the girls at the counter turn away in disappointment, while Marie frowns. She probably has a lot of questions right now.

"When's your exam?" he asks, nodding at our exam preparation.

"In an hour and a half."

"Are you well prepared?" he asks, as if still following a script.

"Why? Want to test me?" I tease, leaning into him. As far as I know, Sébastien has never studied anything.

Across the table, Gaby raises an eyebrow. I give her a sharp look and she immediately relaxes. Instead of staring at Sébastien, she leans forward in interest. "It's so nice to finally meet the man behind the flowers. And the champagne." Her acting far surpasses mine.

Sébastien smiles sheepishly. "I take it you both enjoyed that?" He looks at me for confirmation.

Gaby bursts out laughing, drawing another puzzled look from Marie. "Oh, very much. And now the opera. You're really spoiling my girl. Which, admittedly, she deserves big time."

"What's this about the opera?" Sébastien asks baffled.

"I found two tickets in my letterbox from a secret admirer. Expensive tickets, too".

Sébastien's frown deepens. "I didn't—"

"Think we'd find out?" Gaby says with another laugh. Marie has returned to the table, still looking confused.

"Are you ready to order?" she asks Sébastien, hiding behind her role.

Gaby puts an arm around her hips. "Hey chérie. I don't think you've met Séb. He's Alix's new beau."

"New... What about Gaspar?" she asks, obviously not thinking about the fact a ghost boyfriend would be kind of difficult to explain in a new relationship.

Tight-lipped, I reply, "He's gone."

Marie's face softens. "I see." She turns back to Sébastien. "Can I get you something?"

"A cappuccino, please."

When Marie returns to the counter, Gaby gives me another pointed look. I mouth an apology before returning to the subject at hand. "I had an unexpected visitor," I tell Sébastien, hoping he will understand. "He invited me to the opera this Saturday on behalf of someone there. I assume it involves a favour."

He doesn't like it. "I don't think that's a good idea." He leans in and lowers his voice, his breath caressing my ear. "What about keeping your head down?"

"It's the opera. Are you telling me—" *GoPol has people there too?* I want to ask, but Marie returns with Sébastien's drink.

"Here you go." She places the cup in front of me. "Did I hear that right? You invited Alix to the opera? Fancy!" She grins at me encouragingly and returns to the counter as new customers come in.

I'm too intrigued by the mysterious letter. Maybe it's the foolish, desperate hope that somehow Gaspar is behind it all. "I've already told my family we're going. Maman wants to meet you. Properly. And a certain couple was there too."

Sébastien looks at me as if I'm torturing him. "Alix..."

"Please. It could be..." Now it's me who leans in and whispers in Sébastien's ear. "What if it's a message from Dix?" Now that I've said it, it actually makes a lot of sense. As a whisper ghost, he has more control over the physical world. Maybe not enough to write a letter, but he could influence someone who could. I can see Dix reaching out to me that way, too. Besides, he probably likes the opera as much as his living half. If so, I hope Dix won't mind if I bring Sébastien along. Then again, who else would he think I'd bring?

As I lean back, my eyes meet Théo's, who has stepped up to the counter. Ugh. Is he following me, too, or something?

I put my arms around Sébastien's neck and look deep into his blue eyes with an over-ambitious smile. "Please say yes."

Sébastien blushes under my gaze. Fortunately, he knows how to play the game. "Well, if it means that much to you, of course I'll take you to the opera. When's the performance?"

"Saturday at seven."

"I'll pick you up at five."

I manage an award-worthy squeal and kiss his forehead for good measure. Surely that's enough to get the message across to Théo. When I sit down again, I only see the back of him as he leaves the café with a coffee-to-go.

Still flustered, Sébastien drinks his coffee. Meanwhile, Gaby looks as if she's about to burst out laughing. When she catches my eye, she blurts out: "You two are so cute.

I throw my pencil case at her, making her giggle.

Later, as we both hurry to our exam, she says, "Be careful what you do. That boy is either a world-class actor or he's actually in love with you."

CHAPTER 7

With all the exams this week, Saturday comes around faster than I'm ready for. I keep thinking about the mysterious tickets. Are they from Gaspar? Are they from Dix? Is it some elaborate trap from GoPol? Or is it all just wishful thinking and I'm being asked for a simple favour? Not that I wish for the latter.

Odile has promised to help me get ready, but all she does is create content for Instagram by having Malou pick out my clothes. I give Malou a lot of credit, but selecting outfits is not her forte. "I'm not going to wear a sundress."

"But Malou would look so cute in it." Odile picks Malou up and cuddles her. "Don't worry, ma puce. Auntie Odi will make you a pretty sundress. And a hat."

"Yeah, I won't wear a hat to the opera." Before Odile can stop me, I grab the floor-length midnight blue dress with the sculpted bust and get ready while my sister plays with Malou.

I apply a subtle amount of make-up and brush out my waves before choosing a cream cardigan to complement the look and keep me warm. Finally, I turn to Odile. "What do you think?"

"Wow. You're really into him, aren't you?"

"What?" I blurt out, shocked she would even suggest it. Then I remember I'm *supposed* to be into Sébastien. "Oh, well, it's the opera."

Odile smiles mischievously. "Oh yes, can't be underdressed there." She picks up Malou and holds her in front of me. "Mummy's got a date with a hot guy. Wish her luck she doesn't embarrass herself."

Malou is very uninterested in my upcoming event and squirms in Odile's grip. I gently take her back to her cage, where she immediately goes for a drink. "I can't embarrass myself anymore. Not by talking to people who aren't there. Although I suppose he can see them, too, so it wouldn't be embarrassing in the first place." Then the rest of Odile's words sink in. "You think Sébastien is hot?"

"Don't you?" Odile asks, as if I'm out of my mind.

I guess I've never looked at him like that, unavailable as I was. When we first met, I was in shock, and then I had a million questions. Sébastien's supposed hotness has been very low on my list of priorities.

Just then the door rings. "He's here." Suddenly I'm all nerves. Our last date was pleasantly unromantic. Just two friends walking through a cemetery. This is in a different league. Sure, friends go to the opera all the time, but an unmarried couple in a private box? Both looking their best? That sounds like a real date.

Odile looks at me and laughs. "Come on! Don't keep him waiting. Open the door."

But it's too late. My parents get there first and I already hear him climbing the stairs. I burst out of my room just as he comes through the door.

Some of the snow falling outside is still clinging to his shoulders and melting in his hair. His cheeks are slightly flushed from the cold and somehow his blue eyes sparkle. And to top it all off, he's wearing a suit. A very well-fitting suit.

Okay, yes, he's hot. Objectively speaking, of course.

"Salut. Ça va?" He greets my parents, who look positively delighted to make his acquaintance, even though they've both seen him before. Then he turns to me, and our cheeks meet. He really *is* cold.

The difference in temperature makes me say, "I'll get my coat."

"Would you like to come in? I can make some coffee," Maman offers.

As obedient as ever, Sébastien waits for my cue. I have a feeling the evening at the opera will be difficult enough. We don't need our first meeting with the parents on the same night. "We have a show to catch."

"It'll only take a few minutes," Maman tells me.

"Is the coffee ready?" I ask doubtfully as I slip into my winter boots. They're not the most elegant shoes to go with my dress, but I'm less likely to slip and *embarrass* myself, as Odile said.

Papa laughs and puts an arm around Maman's shoulders. "Let them go, Marguerite." He nods at me. "Have a good night."

"You, too," Sébastien says with a friendly smile as I put on my coat and wrap a scarf around my neck.

Just as we're about to step out the door, Maman calls after me, "Text me if you're not planning on coming home."

"Maman!" I can't believe she said that in front of Sébastien. "I'll be home."

Although our apartment is nice and warm, Sébastien's cheeks have turned even redder. "I promise to bring her home right after."

What am I? Sixteen?

Papa coughs, hiding a smile, while my mother grins and waves. "Have fun!"

I shove Sébastien out the door before he can further put his foot in his mouth, closing the door behind me. "You know I'm a grown woman, right?"

The colour in his cheeks intensifies. "I've never met anyone's parents before."

To be fair, that's my fault. I didn't write him a script for tonight. "It's okay. It was kind of cute."

Sébastien swallows. "I forgot to tell you how beautiful you look."

"Seriously, it's okay. The meeting went well." If anything, my parents will think we're adorable. Nothing about our interaction suggests this is just an act. "Let's go. We can worry about how long I should stay out after the show."

CHAPTER 8

Half an hour later we arrive at the Palais Garnier. The good thing about winter is that it's already dark, so the neo-classical building is lit up in rich golden tones. People are milling around the entrance, chatting in small groups or waiting for others to join them. Traffic is backed up as taxis drop off visitors and hawkers sell hot treats. Everyone looks gorgeous today and there's an excited buzz in the air.

The last time I was here was probably when I was a teenager. My fondest memory is even further back, when I was five or six. My grandmother took me and Hélène to a Christmas performance of The Nutcracker. It was during the day, and we sat somewhere in the second tier, far from the stage. But I remember the opulence, the excitement, and the beautiful dancers.

But no amount of previous visits prepares you for entering the opera house. The doors are manned by ushers who open them for us with a welcoming smile. We climb up a vestibule with statues of famous composers, then another for the ticket and programme sellers. None of them gets more than a glance from me as we enter the auditorium that houses the Grand Staircase. Slightly wider at the bottom, it narrows to the central landing before splitting into two sets of stairs leading up to the tiers and boxes. White marble steps on red marble balusters resting on green marble plinths, it's more a centrepiece than a functional feature, a stage in itself for the patrons. Several balconies on the first floor, surrounded by marble columns, overlook the staircase. It's practically intended for a grand entrance.

Above the Grand Staircase hangs the chandelier, sparkling with the reflection of a thousand lights. Around it, the ceiling is a little jarring. While the rest of the opera house is covered in gold and marble, rich, warm, earthy tones, the fresco above us is decked in bright colours. Red, blue, green, and yellow, it depicts famous composers and Parisian landmarks.

"It was repainted in the sixties by Marc Chagall," says Sébastien, noticing my stare. "It caused quite a stir at the time."

I can imagine why. People love what they know, and this painting is a radical departure from the classical nature of the rest of the opera house. Amused, I turn to him. "Historical facts—way to talk dirty to a girl." This girl at least. When Sébastien coughs in a fit of nerves, I laugh. "I'm kidding."

"Shall I hand in your coat?" he asks, painfully formal.

"Thank you." I shrug off my coat and scarf and hand them to him. As he takes both, he whispers, "This is a great place to practice your new skills."

Surprised, I look around once more. A lot of people are milling about. There are ushers on every level and servers with trays of drinks. And, of course, there are tonight's guests in their finest ensembles. Come to think of it, there are a few who've really outdone themselves. I see a man with long tails and a cylinder, and a woman in a dress that would've made Marie Antoinette jealous. Another woman's standing in the middle of the landing of the Grand Staircase, singing a short aria to her adoring fans on the balcony. Since I'm pretty sure the actual performers don't have time to entertain the crowd, it's safe to say her glory days are far behind her.

Sébastien returns to my side. "So?"

"There are so many... *old* people here." An elderly lady gives me the stink-eye as she leans on her husband. "I didn't mean..." I try to apologise, but she wrinkles her nose at me and walks on.

Sébastien laughs quietly next to me. "There are. Old employees, patrons, dancers, singers. It's a lively place."

"Or deadly."

He laughs again. "True. Shall we grab a drink and find our box?" he asks, offering me his arm. Something's different tonight. Sébastien is more relaxed, more like Dix. It's as if this place has a healing effect on him. Maybe it's because all this art and splendour couldn't be further from the rigid structure of the ghost police. I quite enjoy this new side of him. It's good to see him letting go a little.

I link my arm with his and nod in the direction of the Grand Staircase. "Lead the way."

Watching the opera from a box is a very different experience to watching it from the first or second tier. Firstly, you can actually see the expressions on the singers' faces. Now it's not just their songs and movements that tell the story, but their faces, too. Secondly, we can see the whole stage. No one's sitting in front of us, blocking out part of the play. And finally, it's like being in our own little world, separate from everyone else.

When we arrived at the box, a bottle of champagne and a box of chocolates were waiting for us. I asked our personal usher, but she had no idea who'd left them there and suggested it might have been the managers' treat. Could it be? Could the opera manager have invited us? If so, they don't make themselves known to us. Nor are we disturbed by any of the ghosts.

The opera itself is a story as old as time. Medée tells the story of Medea, years after she helped Jason steal the Golden Fleece and given him children, only to be abandoned for another woman: Dircé. As he prepares for his wedding, Medea appears and begs him to return to her. When he refuses, she curses him. I'm completely invested in her pain, and even shed a tear during one of her magnificent arias. The actress playing Dircé is just as good, if not better, and I feel it's more a story about these two women getting the short end of the stick than it is about Jason.

It's not until the interval after the second act that I think of my mysterious benefactor. Sébastien and I remain seated for a while, thinking they might approach us in the privacy of the box, but the door never opens. As much as I love this evening, I'm confused. The ghost in my room stressed the importance of my presence. But there's nothing strange about this performance. Sure, the stage is busier than it would be for people who can't see ghosts, but the ghostly performers are just as committed as the living ones, adding to the play rather than detracting from it.

"Maybe they're waiting in the foyer," I say, a few minutes into the interval.

Sébastien shrugs. "We can have a look."

As soon as we get up, the door opens, but it's just our usher doing her job. She smiles and points us towards the nearest bar. I wonder if she's a ghost, but that's literally impossible and just shows how much practice I need. Despite myself, I ask Sébastien as soon as we're out of earshot.

"The usher? No, she's very much alive. Besides, if she were a—" I elbow him. "Hush."

We're walking along the balustrade when I notice a familiar head of hair in the crowd on the Grand Staircase. It's the same shade of brown as mine, but hers is elegantly pinned up. Hélène is here—alongside Cédric, of course. "I can't believe it. They must've bought their tickets as soon as I said I was going."

Sébastien frowns heavily as he steps onto the balustrade and watches the couple. "I don't like this."

"That makes two of us." I take a deep breath before I ask my next question. "Cédric mentioned he was being promoted. Has he been made a ghost whisperer?"

"Not yet." Sébastien rolls his eyes. "He's been given a lowly trainee position downstairs. His main job is still with the gendarmes, but he gets to do some data processing."

I snort. "Totally worth exploiting his sister-in-law for."

Sébastien looks at me worriedly. "Unfortunately, that appears to be the family standard. For what it's worth, I'm sorry. Cédric is an ass."

"Oh, I've got a lot more choice words for him." And *Hélène*. She's not even married to him yet and I already feel like I've lost a sister. Cédric has her completely wrapped around his finger and washed her mind. I watch the two of them being all lovey-dovey below us and feel my stomach turn. "Let's go back to the box."

If someone wanted to talk to me, they should've made themselves known.

The third act is where all the drama takes place. Medea has her two children kidnapped with the intention of murdering them in revenge, but first she has to make sure the new wife won't survive the wedding. One of the two gifts she'd left her in the previous act was a poisoned wedding dress. Dircé puts it on and admires herself in the mirror.

"Here it comes," says a voice to my right.

At first, I think it's Sébastien, but he's sitting on my other side. I quickly look over my shoulder before the screams on stage distract me. Dircé is dying, writhing dramatically on the floor and screaming. I'm not familiar with the play, so I don't know if there should've been a song or a dance, but this modern interpretation of her death is incredibly uncomfortable to watch. A bit over the top for my taste. Surely, we don't need to watch her die for so long.

The actress playing a maid tends to Dircé, and at first it looks very much like part of the play, but then she suddenly calls out to the crowd, "Someone call an ambulance, quick!"

Is that still in the script? It's hard to tell with these modern operas. The subject matter may be old-fashioned, but they also had Jason flying a WWII fighter jet instead of sailing on the Argonaut.

"Merde!" Sébastien's up. "Come on!"

"What? What's happening?" More actors have gathered around the fallen Dircé. The orchestra has stopped playing and a murmur rises from the crowd. Cold fear runs down my spine. Could it be?

"Help!" cries the maid again. "Why is no one helping her?"

The actor playing Jason kneels beside Dircé, checks her vital signs and immediately starts CPR. I'm still clinging to the hope that this is all part of the production, because the alternative... the alternative is too grim to contemplate.

"We have to go," Sébastien urges, although I have no idea where he needs to go so suddenly.

And then I see it. Jason's still doing compressions, but the body on the stage is no longer the only Dircé. Her ghost is standing next to her, looking terribly confused.

The poor woman just died.

Chapter 9

T urns out that when Sébastien witnesses a death, he switches into police mode. We leave the box only to head towards the stage entrance. On the way, he notifies the emergency services and waves his badge to let us backstage. Gone is the shy gentleman who accompanied me today. In his place is the confident GoPol officer I first met. This is his world, his expertise, and I'm just tagging along because I have nowhere else to be.

And because this is what I was meant to see.

I swallow hard as I remember the voice that spoke to me seconds before the Dircé actress died. It was a man's voice, and that's all I can remember before the stage demanded my attention. My brain refuses to follow the logical train of thought, the implications of it all, but I push on, knowing it's going to be important. I can't get the dying woman out of my mind. How long we watched her die. It felt like an eternity.

The voice knew. The voice *knew*. I hold onto that fact and push the disturbing images aside. Whoever invited me here knew what was going to happen and that means... that means, it was murder.

Shocked, I stop short. A woman was murdered, right in front of us. And I was invited to witness it.

Was it the killer who invited me? I have absolutely no connection with the murdered actress or anyone else on stage, so why did he choose me? It's far more likely a ghost came to me after witnessing the devious plot. But why not tell me, so I could stop it? Did I miss the signs? Did I ignore the wrong ghost today? Could I have saved that woman?

"Alix?" Sébastien has noticed I'm no longer following him. He takes one look at my face and nods sharply. "You don't need to watch this. Wait down here, okay?"

He turns away, but I grab his arm and pour out all my thoughts. "The ghost. He was there. In the box. He warned me. He knew this would happen. It's a murder. I was supposed to stop it. I—"

Sébastien turns to me and puts his hands on my face, forcing me to look deep into his eyes. "Whatever's happening here is not your fault. Okay?"

I give him the smallest of nods. "Okay," I whisper.

He's about to say something else when the door opens behind us, and Cédric and Hélène join us backstage. Like Sébastien, Cédric flashes his badge. "You."

Sébastien lets go of me. "I was here first."

"There's enough room on the stage for two policemen."

"You're not needed here."

Cédric snorts. "I think you'll find I'm superior to you."

Sébastien's face darkens. "Not at GoPol."

"Ah, but this isn't a GoPol case, is it?" Cédric gives Sébastien an ugly smile. Apparently, he's not wearing his kind and caring mask today. "A woman just died on stage, possibly murdered in a sinister 'life imitating art' moment. There are no ghosts involved, except the one who's just been created. So there's nothing for you to do here, is there?"

I see the storm inside Sébastien. He doesn't want to work on this case with Cédric, but he doesn't want to give up either. Not after I told him about my mysterious benefactor's involvement. "As you just said, a ghost has been created. Unless something's changed, I'm the only one who can question her."

This hits Cédric where it hurts. He sneers at his cousin. "We don't work with ghost testimonies."

I find that terribly short-sighted, but who am I to criticise GoPol's responsibilities?

Sébastien has had enough of this pissing contest, turns on his heel, and heads for the stage. Cédric, not to be left behind, hurries after him, leaving me alone with Hélène.

Awkward.

For a few heartbeats, neither of us says anything. My thoughts are with the poor woman who died and the mysterious person who wanted to make sure I saw her murder. But Hélène's presence is hard to ignore. She looks straight ahead, her back so straight you could hang pictures on it, her arms folded across her chest, radiating discomfort and anger.

I decide to address the elephant in the room. "Fancy seeing you here. Today."

"We've had these tickets for months," is her icy reply.

I don't believe her and snort.

Hélène rolls her eyes and inhales, her nostrils flaring. "It's our third anniversary."

Well, how should I know? Still, I can think of better things to do than celebrate my first kiss or whatever by shadowing my little sister. "Congratulations," I reply sourly.

We continue to stand there in silence, both of us looking up at the stairs to the stage. From the sounds of it, the auditorium is being cleared. Then a couple of paramedics burst through the door and hurry past us. Cédric is attempting to do some crowd control with the group of actors still on stage, while Sébastien has moved to the side and is talking to Dircé's ghost near the curtains.

"So, you're with Sébastien now?" my sister says after a while, the question so loaded it almost buries me.

"You have a problem with that?"

"No. At least this one's alive."

As if her fiancé hadn't taken Gaspar away from me. "Lucky me."

A few of the actors filter out, all of them in total shock, while the management enters the stage with a group of uniformed officers. But it's not just the living who gather here. Several ghosts pass by, attracted by the scandal of it all.

"It's just like 1896. They tried to kill the diva then, too," says an old patron.

"The chandelier fell on the audience. I should know, it killed me," says another woman.

I ignore them both, despite the terribly interesting conversation they're having.

"The Phantom strikes again," says one man, his eyes wide with horror.

Of course I've heard of The Phantom of the Opera. I even read the book when I was fourteen or fifteen and officially in my gothic novel era. But even though the book presents the case of the Phantom with a series of evidence, slowly revealing the very non-ghostly explanation behind the terror, there has never been any real proof of a man hiding in the walls of the opera house. Living or dead.

A lady in a fancy dress admonishes the man. "Do not speak of him."

"Mademoiselle Dubois."

I turn to face an unfamiliar man. He's an inch or two shorter than me, with floppy grey hair and an unfashionable moustache. His dark bug eyes look at me with great relief. "It is an honour to have you visit my house today. Alas, under such unfortunate circumstances."

He's a ghost. Ghost. Ghost. I continue to turn my head, as if I've suddenly developed an interest in the interior design—fading frescoes and more columns—before I sigh and look back at the stage. "How much longer do you think they'll be?"

Hélène snorts. "As long as it takes."

"My name is Charles Garnier," the ghost says, moving directly into my line of sight. "I'm sorry I didn't greet you earlier. I was not informed of your visit beforehand, you see, but this is truly a fortunate occurrence."

Staring at someone as if they don't exist is much harder than I thought it'd be when they won't stop bothering me. I know, of course, that this is the man who built this great opera house, hence the whole "my house" and the name of the building. And as excited as I'd normally be to make the acquaintance of someone so illustrious, I can't acknowledge him. Not here, next to Hélène, close to the man who betrayed me in the first place.

My lack of response or recognition doesn't bother Garnier much. He rambles on, apologising for disturbing my evening. "Well, in my time I would have invited you into the subscribers' foyer, but I'm afraid I can't offer anything anymore, and they've redesigned the room for their tours. It's just not what it used to be, I'm afraid. But there's still magic. A lot of it, in fact."

I wonder if he has a point and shift uncomfortably on my feet. Staring blindly ahead is making my eyes itch. Am I still acting reasonably normal, or will my sister be on to me any minute?

"Well, I'd like to apologise by inviting you to one of our more intimate performances. Dead people only, if you know what I mean. We have the likes of Pélissier and Le Maure, when they're not at each other's throats again."

Oh, how I'd love to attend a performance by some of the greatest opera singers Paris has ever seen. The very fact that they're still performing is so interesting. I wonder if they do it in the early hours of the morning when no one else is around. I have a million questions. Unfortunately, I can't ask any of them. I have to let this one go. If only Garnier would take the hint.

"Well, maybe not tonight." He frowns slightly. "The thing is, Mademoiselle Dubois, we could use your help."

And there it is. A favour.

"You see—"

"There you are." I do something incredibly rude and walk straight into Garnier as Sébastien comes down the stairs. The architect stumbles aside and looks at me in shock. I bet no one's jostled him aside in the last hundred and fifty years. But Cédric is right behind Sébastien, and I can't afford to show any weakness. "Did you find out who did it?"

"You just ran over a ghost," Sébastien points out, adding to my ruse.

Suitably flustered, I turn in the wrong direction and apologise.

"The other way," says Sébastien with an admirable sigh.

My cheeks flush with embarrassment. "Oh, um... the woman. Dircé. Have you found out what happened?"

Sébastien puts his hand on my back and leads me away from the stairs. "I'm afraid I can't give you any details. It's an ongoing investigation, you know?" His eyes tell another story. I'll just have to save my questions for later. "I've offered to talk to the ghosts here, but the police have refused my help." He gives Cédric a dirty look before his gaze wanders and lands on Garnier instead. "Let's go home."

Just then, a weeping woman is led down the stairs. Blond hair, blue eyes, the hint of burn marks on her neck. Surprised, I realise I know her. She was our usher this evening. When did she come on stage and why is she crying so much? Many people are in tears, shocked by the night's events, but this one is beside herself.

"Did she know the victim?" I ask Sébastien.

He sighs and nods. "That's Natalie Visse, the soprano's little sister."

I can't help it and look over at my sister in Cédric's arms, feeling the tiniest pang of regret. Then her icy gaze hits me and the sensation fades. For a split second, my eyes fall on poor ignored Charles Garnier. "Let's go."

CHAPTER 10

G arnier follows us outside, having at least taken the hint. Outside the opera house, chaos reigns. People are discussing what has happened, the police are cordoning off the building, and reporters have arrived, eager to get the first scoop. There's no chance of getting a taxi. Or so I think.

Turns out being a GoPol officer has its advantages. A flash of Sébastien's badge and a few apologies, and we're allowed to skip the queue and take the first taxi that pulls up. Like the gentleman he is, he opens the door for me before telling the driver: "19 rue Balzac, please.

That's not my address. Curious and with a good deal of nerves, I wait until the door's closed and the taxi's moving before I ask him. "We're going to your place?"

"I thought we could use a bit of privacy."

It makes sense. Perfect sense, in fact. A lot has happened tonight, and we need to be able to talk freely. If we go to my place, we can be certain at least Odile will have her ear pressed against the wall, and a public place is even worse. Still, I've never been in a man's apartment before, let alone the one I'm supposed to be dating.

It's for a good cause, I tell my fraying nerves. This will only strengthen our act. There'll be no doubt about it now, and the sooner we've convinced everyone that I'm harmless and sufficiently distracted, the sooner we can start looking for Dix and Gaspar.

When the taxi stops in the rue Balzac, Charles Garnier is already waiting at the door. The house itself is near the Arc de Triomphe. I saw glimpses of it as we drove down the street, but it's blocked by the house itself as we get out. Instead, the windows look out onto a pretty little park, its branches covered in snow.

Sébastien pays the driver before opening the door for me. We both ignore Garnier, not knowing who might be watching. It's only nine o'clock and there's still light in some of the apartments in the building. The building itself is quite similar to mine. There's no elevator, just a staircase that winds in a square to the top floor. Sébastien's apartment is on the fifth floor, just under the roof, and it turns out to be almost as big as my family's flat.

"GoPol pays well," I say as he lets me in.

"Spy work usually does. It's supposed to keep you loyal and incorruptible. Not that it keeps the corruption itself at bay," he adds in a bitter mumble. With a sigh, he turns on the light and drops his key in a bowl in the hallway. "Sorry about the mess. I didn't exactly plan for visitors."

I don't know what I expected from his flat, which is basically a bachelor pad, but messy is not the word I would have used to describe what I see. Everything looks clean and tidy, apart from a few papers on the coffee table and an empty takeaway box.

Sébastien clears both up in half a minute and offers me a seat on the couch. "Would you like some wine?"

"Sure." I sit down on the couch and take in my surroundings. We've skipped two rooms in the hallway and settled into a living room with an open kitchen. A small balcony is attached to one of the floor-to-ceiling windows, with just enough room for two wrought iron chairs and a tiny table. It's mostly covered in snow at the moment, but with a view of the park outside, it's a pretty romantic spot.

The living room itself is rather unspectacular. There's a big TV and the aforementioned coffee table and couch. In one corner is a dining table with two chairs and a small pile of files. Against one wall is a bookshelf filled with textbooks and classic novels. On the other hangs certificates. Apparently, he graduated at the top of his class at police school and has received the highest honours in several martial arts. There's not a single photograph. The most surprising thing is a row of potted plants in front of the other set of windows.

"You've got a green thumb?"

"Inherited from the previous owner. They just keep growing."

True to his word, the plants are tall and bushy and green. They look very healthy, indeed.

"Can we talk now?" Charles Garnier asks, rubbing his moustache. "It's quite important."

Immediately reminded of the gruesome murder we witnessed, I swallow hard. "Is the apartment safe?"

Sébastien comes back with two glasses and a Merlot. "As safe as it can be. It's not necessarily ghost-proof, but I'm not under surveillance or anything like that." He smiles softly. "You can talk to him now."

Apparently, it's only me who needs to talk to the ghost. I don't care. I'm just glad I can finally look Garnier in the eye. "'Hi, I'm so sorry I had to pretend not to see you, Monsieur Garnier. Things are a bit... precarious at the moment. How can I help you?"

Beside me, Sébastien clears his throat. "Shouldn't we ask a few questions first?"

"Questions?"

He gives Garnier his stern police look. "Were you the one who invited Alix?"

"Invited her?" Garnier frowns. "I had no idea Mademoiselle Dubois was coming to the opera tonight, but I'm glad she did."

That's right. For a moment I'd forgotten about the fancy tickets. But if Garnier hadn't orchestrated their delivery, who did? Who wanted me there tonight of all nights?

"Why?" Sébastien asks rather harshly, still in interrogation mode. "What do you want with her?"

"Something is stirring in the opera. An unnatural presence with a sinister mind."

That doesn't sound good. "A sinister mind?"

"The living would say the opera is haunted, but you and I know that's not the case, or rather that our ghosts aren't the problem here. Sure, we hang around and use the facilities, but we're very accommodating and plan our rehearsals and performances around the schedule of the living."

"You really put on ghost operas?" I can't help it, I'm painfully fascinated by all this.

Garnier beams at me. "As I said, we would love for you to come and see us. It'd be my pleasure."

"A woman died tonight," Sébastien reminds us in a tired voice. "On stage. The autopsy hasn't confirmed it yet, but judging by the dramatic way she died, we can be pretty sure she was murdered."

"That's why I'm here," Garnier explains, his face pure misery. "I'm afraid this is just the latest climax of the evil within our walls. In recent years, ghosts as well as the living have been harassed. There have been a disproportionate number of accidents, and someone is tampering with the systems. Mass cancellations of subscriptions, missing payments. It makes the opera look sloppy, even scandalous. Mademoiselle Dubois, I'm asking you to help me save the reputation of my house. Imagine if we were forced to close. Paris needs its opera. We need it."

I didn't know the Palais Garnier was in such dire straits. I can't really imagine anyone would consider shutting it down, it's too much of a landmark, but then again I haven't been following the news closely. In this economy, who knows? The arts are usually the first to feel the pinch. "That's terrible. I—"

"She can't," says Sébastien before I can agree to this favour. Not that I have any idea what I'm even supposed to do. "I'm sure there are plenty of people who will fight to keep the opera open. Alix can't help you."

Miffed that he thinks he can speak for me, I glare at him. "Don't I have a say in this?"

"Alix, please. The last thing you need is to interfere with an ongoing murder investigation that's already attracted Cédric's attention. Remember, you need to keep a low profile."

"Can you tell me more about this presence?" I ask Garnier, completely ignoring Sébastien's sensible words.

Garnier looks back and forth between us, as if deciding who's in charge here. Then he shrugs his shoulders. "No one has seen anything, not even us ghosts, but people have reported hearing voices and things being moved. Nails have come loose, paint has been spilt, costumes ruined. I think it is an evil spirit, someone who hates the opera with every fibre of his being".

"And you want Alix to expel this evil presence?" Sébastien asks in disbelief.

"She has a reputation."

"I do?" Last time I checked, I could talk to ghosts, not hunt them down.

Garnier looks at me with all the hope in the world. "You have broken the power of Jacques de Molay."

"I didn't mean to. And I had help. Lots of help."

"Then take all the help you need. I will tell every ghost in the opera house to help you. And we'll do all we can to make sure the living are open to it, too. We have some influence over them." His shoulders slump. "Please. I'm afraid tonight was just the beginning of our nightmare."

Before I can make up my mind, Sébastien decides to take the lead again. "We'll think about it."

Garnier crumples under Sébastien's clear dismissal. "I hope you change your mind." Then he gets up and floats out onto the balcony. A moment later he's gone.

"Was that really necessary?" I hiss at Sébastien. "Didn't you see how important this was to him?"

Sébastien pours the wine, awfully calm about the disturbing news we've just received. "I meant what I said. This isn't the time for one of your favours."

"This isn't just a favour," I argue. "Don't you want to get to the bottom of this? A woman just died."

"And the police are on it," says Sébastien, not unkindly. "Ghosts can't kill people."

"Unless they're ghost whisperers."

For some reason that gets me a sharp look instead. "True, but the soprano wasn't. I spoke to her, and she was extremely confused, not just by her death, but by all the ghosts on stage and her own condition. It was simply murder. Living on living."

"Did she tell you who killed her?"

"She couldn't even tell me *what* killed her. Most people go into shock. All that pain and transition often blurs the death until it comes back later."

It reminds me of Gaspar, who didn't quite realise he was dead for the longest time—partly because of me.

Sébastien's face softens. "As much as I hate it, Cédric was right. This is not a GoPol case. Let's leave the investigation to the police, okay?" He offers me the wine glass as if it were a peace offering.

"Don't you want to know for yourself?" I ask, taking the glass and sipping at the wine. "At the opera, you almost jumped on stage when it happened. You fought with Cédric to be first on the scene and even tried to pull rank."

Sébastien blushes. "That was out of line. I wasn't thinking straight."

"You weren't?" He looked pretty calm to me, a professional in his field.

"When I saw Cédric... I wanted to punch him. I wanted to punch him so hard he'll need a plastic surgeon to attend his wedding," he confesses.

My heart warms, whether from the very good Merlot or from Sébastien's confession, I can't tell. His relationship with Cédric had never been good, but now it seems to have deteriorated further, and I can't help but think it's because of me.

I lean forward and lick the wine from my lips. "So, why give in now?"

Sébastien swallows. "Because it's too dangerous. I know you're used to helping all these ghosts, but it's too risky. My father is still on your case and nothing Garnier has said has filled me with confidence that this is safe. If he's right, and this is a ghost of Molay's calibre, I want you as far away from them as possible."

"I don't know whether that's sweet or condescending."

His eyes widen. "I just want you to be safe."

"You asked me to help you find Dix."

"Yes, but in a safe way." He looks utterly miserable. "Do you really think they need you? That they can't handle their own problems? You don't owe them anything."

He reminds me of Gaby. And like Gaby, he's going to have to learn that I can't just turn a blind eye when people come to me for help. "It's not about owing anyone anything. If there's something I can do to help, I have to try. They don't have anyone else."

Of course, Sébastien doesn't understand. He's never dealt with the needs of ghosts before. "Alix, please."

I put my glass on the table and take his hands to comfort him. "Look, I understand that maybe this isn't the best idea right now. Believe me, I know that, but remember, someone invited me here today. Someone made sure I had a front row seat to the drama."

"It could be coincidence," says Sébastien, although he frowns heavily.

"Maybe, but remember what I told you? Just before Dircé died—"

"Emanuelle Visse."

"Emanuelle Visse," I say, memorising the name. "Just before she died, the moment she put on the dress, there was this voice. 'Here it comes,' it said. It was a man's voice. I didn't see anyone, but there was someone behind me. Someone *knew* Emanuelle was going to die on stage. And they made sure I was there to see it."

After listening intently, Sébastien sighs. "You know that only worries me more."

I'm oddly charmed by his interest in my safety. "Me, too, but if there's one thing I've learnt from my disaster at GoPol, it's that I'm not going to sit around waiting for the hammer to fall. I need to know who set me up."

"It could be the killer," warns Sébastien.

I'm well aware of that and take a deep breath. "It could be. Whoever it is, they, the murderer, and this evil presence that's frightening the ghosts are all connected."

Another sigh follows. "Very well, we'll have a look, but you must promise me to be careful. You can't be seen talking to ghosts."

"Understood."

"And we'll do it together."

I can't stop a smile from forming on my lips. "Of course, I couldn't do it without my alibi."

CHAPTER 11

Although I'm eager to act, Sébastien warns me to wait until the dust has settled. At the moment, the police are still at the opera house and there hasn't even been an autopsy report yet. Sébastien promised to keep me updated, while I had to promise to keep my head down and concentrate on the rest of my exams. At the same time, the death is all over the news.

Gaby and I sit in the Sorbonne library with the paper. We're supposed to be studying, but of course my best friend hasn't missed the fact the murder happened while I was at the opera house.

"Are you alright?"

I had nightmares both nights since Emanuelle's death. The fact I thought it was part of her act freaks me out. Could she have been saved if someone had realised at once? "I'm fine." Gaby raises an eyebrow. "Obviously it was quite disturbing, but I didn't see the body. Not up close anyway."

"The news says there's an ongoing murder investigation." Gaby points to the article. "I don't really get it, though. She wasn't shot or stabbed."

"She put on a poisoned dress."

"In the play, yes, but... do you think that's it? That someone poisoned the dress? How would that even work?"

I shrug. "No idea. A contact poison, I suppose. Look, we didn't get to do the historical poison course." Unfortunately, they took it out of the programme the year before we could've signed up. I'd really been looking forward to it.

"Do you think they used a historical poison?" Gaby's far too invested in this. I blame her obsession with true-crime podcasts.

"Have poisons changed that much?"

"Oh, you have no idea!" Gaby's face lights up. "There are so many compounds now you can only make in a chemical lab. Heck, half my cleaning products are poisons."

Fair point. This probably isn't some fancy arsenic murder. "We don't even know if it *was* poison. Maybe there were needles in the dress. Maybe she *was* stabbed." I try to remember the scene. Her handmaiden was helping her with the dress. It'd be a bold murder—live on stage—but not beyond the realms of possibility.

"Are you talking about the murder at the opera?" Suddenly, Théo, who's been sitting with his friends at the table behind us, turns and switches seats. Of course, now the rest of his posse's interested too.

"Alix was there," Gaby says proudly.

"They don't need to know that," I hiss, but it's too late. The words are out, and now the whole group switches tables and lean in, eager for gossip.

"You went to the opera?" Théo asks, as if it's way out of my natural habitat.

"I had a date, yes."

Théo leans back and flicks his hand. "With that blonde hotshot?"

I don't know why Théo's suddenly taken an interest in my dating life, but here goes. "His name is Sébastien."

"What about the murder?" asks Léon, one of Théo's friends. "How close were you? Did you see who did it?"

Annoyed, I recount the events of the evening, avoiding any mention of ghosts. This whole interrogation is far too sensational. A woman's just died. On the other hand, none of us had any connection with her, and so I slowly warm to the group dynamic. It's kind of nice not to be the weird outsider for a change.

"This is so messed up," Théo finally says. "My brother's beside himself."

"Your brother?" I didn't even know Théo had a brother—or any siblings.

But he nods. "Laurent. He's the tenor. I don't know what role he was playing or if he was on stage at all, but he knew Emanuelle."

"No way." So much for none of us having any connection with her.

Immediately, the conversation shifts to Théo and he's forced to reveal his inside knowledge of the dynamics at the opera. "I only met her a few times. All I know is that she and Alexandra—that's the other soprano—have quite the rivalry going. They were always fighting over roles and stuff. Laurent often complained about how they make the workplace so toxic, but—"

"Duh!" Léon exclaims. "She's the killer! I bet it was some revenge shit."

Gaby rolls her eyes. "Maybe you should leave the murder investigation to the police."

As the two start to argue, I turn to Théo. "Do you visit your brother often?"

He snorts. "Alix, I work there."

"What?" Somehow, I can't imagine Théo being into drama. Then again, with a brother who's a resident tenor at the Paris Opera, his whole family might be into it.

"It's just a student job. In the archives. Mostly I get to digitise old scores." His smile widens. "It's really cool, actually. Last month I found this little operette that's never been performed. Apparently, the diva at the time refused to appear in it and the whole thing was scrapped three weeks before it was supposed to open".

I'm sure this is all incredibly exciting, but I'm not interested in his work. "Can I visit you?"

"Visit me?"

A plan quickly forms in my head. Théo's the perfect alibi for investigating the opera, even better than Sébastien. No one will notice me if I'm just visiting a friend at work. And he knows the cast and probably half the other staff. If I play my cards right, I can question them about this evil presence. Garnier mentioned there have also been accidents for the living.

"I'd like a tour behind the scenes. The *real* backstage". There are plenty of regular tours for tourists, but I don't want to worry about ditching the guide and getting into trouble for being in places I shouldn't be. It's the opposite of keeping a low profile. Théo's work solves all these problems. "Please."

He stares at me, and I'm suddenly reminded we're not exactly friends. I've just ruined whatever credibility I had left with him. But then I see him swallow and shake his head. "Sure, why not. After exams, okay?"

"Exams!"

Everyone looks up and checks the time. A mad scramble ensues as we pack our things in world record time and rush out the library in a barely disguised hurry.

CHAPTER 12

The rest of the week goes by quickly and soon we're off for a well-earned study break. Personally, I can't believe it's already the middle of February. It means that Gaspar—and Dix—have been gone for seven weeks now, almost as long as we were together. I know life goes on and all that crap, but I feel guilty about it. Like I don't deserve to live my life when he's just... gone.

The worst thing is how little I've done to find him. Somehow the weeks have flown by, and I've kept busy building up my ruse and preparing for exams, but now those are over I'm overcome with guilt. The problem is I have no idea where to start. I've tried calling him and I've visited the site of his accident. The flowers and pictures are gone now. Nothing shows anyone died there, so it's no longer a place of remembrance. I suppose he has a grave somewhere, but I've never asked Gaspar. We rarely talked about his death.

As I hurry past the inconspicuous corner, I promise myself I'll find out where he's buried. That might mean contacting his parents, or maybe I could ask his friend Gustave. Or Marie! I wonder if she knows.

Happy with the plan in my head, I travel to the Panthéon for my shift. During exams I only had to work twice, but now I'm happy to take on more shifts. As I see it, it's more time to spend with my ghosts. Besides, it might be a safer place than even Sébastien's apartment.

I say hello to Philippe, and we have a quick chat about the opera when I notice he's reading another article about it. "Have they found out who did it?"

"Still under investigation," he says. "But it's definitely a murder. How did your exams go?"

"Fine. Nothing too bad, I think." Meanwhile, I button my uniform. "Were you there? You like the opera, don't you?" I keep my presence to myself, not wanting the attention to be repeated.

Philippe snorts at me. "As if I could afford it."

"Didn't you go last year? With your friends or something?"

"Yeah, but that was one time. Very fancy and without any murders on stage." He laughs, as if any of this is the least bit funny. "Kind of creepy how they used a death scene to hide it. As if people wouldn't notice. Did you know someone brought up the Phantom of the Opera?" He shakes his head in disbelief. "Anything for a flashy headline, I suppose."

My mind races. Could it be ghost-related? Garnier blamed some mysterious evil presence, but as Sébastien pointed out, ghosts can't actually kill anyone.

Come to think of it, behind all that mystery, the Phantom of the Opera was a real person with an entirely mundane background. How likely is it someone's hiding in the walls of the opera house these days? Surely, they know all the secret passageways by now.

"Hey," says Philippe, just as I'm about to leave for my first tour. "A man was asking for you on Tuesday."

I freeze, my heart jumping into my throat. "A man?"

"Yeah, strange fellow; very pale, hollow eyes. I honestly thought he was a ghost at first. I asked him if he wanted to join one of your tours and he said he wasn't allowed in here." Philippe makes a face. "Do we currently have anyone banned from the premises? Apart from the two teenagers who tried to deface Rousseau?"

His words send a shiver down my spine. The description doesn't fit anyone I know, but it could be a GoPol whisperer I haven't met yet. The fact he felt he wasn't allowed to enter speaks for itself.

"What did he want?"

"To speak to you. He kept asking me to send you out, but you weren't here, obviously. Then he asked if you were still working here." Philippe scratches his nose. "To be honest, he was just very confused. Maybe he was drunk."

That doesn't sound like a GoPol officer, but maybe it was a ruse. "You didn't say anything to him, did you?"

"Just that if he wanted to enter the Panthéon, he had to pay like everyone else. Don't worry, I didn't give him your phone number or anything like that. So, you don't know who it could be?"

"Doesn't ring a bell, no."

Philippe frowns. "Hm, take care, okay?"

I almost laugh at him. If he knew what I'd been up to lately, he'd realise his advice was a bit late. "Will do. Thanks for the warning."

I don't have much time to think about it while I'm giving tours and tidying up the crypt. Although the ghosts told me they have the power to drive away anyone who wishes me ill, I don't acknowledge their presence until the Panthéon is closed and I'm alone with them. Only then do I open my arms to embrace Petite Alix, who's playing quietly in the lower corner near Victor's tomb. As before, the little girl clings to me as if she's never going to let go.

"It's good to have you back," Victor says, putting a fatherly hand on my shoulder. "Someone emptied half a bottle of Coke into our crypt."

"Ugh. I'll get the cleaning stuff in a minute." At least that'll give me an excuse for staying late. Not that I've ever needed one. "Did anyone come looking for me last week?"

Victor's face darkens. "Several people. Not just last week. We've turned them all away."

And here I thought my ruse with Sébastien was enough to stop the constant surveillance. "Thank you."

"Don't worry, kid. We've got your back."

I hand him Petite Alix and go upstairs to grab the cleaning gear. On the stairs, I find Voltaire and Rousseau locked in another petty fight.

"We may be buried next to each other," Voltaire boasts, "but people come for me, not you."

"Did you hear that, Alix?" Rousseau asks outraged. "He thinks people don't care about me."

"They do," I say placatingly. "I had someone asking so many questions about you on my tour today."

Relieved, as if he doubted himself for a bit, Rousseau turns back to Voltaire. "See. People take an interest in me."

"Because they have no idea who you are," Voltaire shots back.

Eek, I'd better keep out of this one. I grab my stuff and go back downstairs.

As I carefully clean up the sticky spill, I tell the ghosts about the murder at the opera and Garnier's request. "Apparently there's a whole community of ghosts at the opera. They even put on their own shows."

"Of course they do," Voltaire says, slightly irritated.

I stare at him. "Of course." For a moment I forgot who I was talking to. "Have you been to the shows?"

Voltaire seems to grow three centimetres, looking very smug. "As you may know, I'm a proud supporter of the arts, especially the opera. My good friend Frederic used to ask me a lot of questions about the operas being performed in Paris and to send him new compositions for his flute play. That's the Prussian king I'm talking about."

"I know," I say gently, not bothered by his boast. If my best friend was a foreign king, I'd be boasting about it, too. "That reminds me, Monsieur Garnier mentioned Mesdames Pélissier and Le Maure were both regular performers."

"Marie Pélissier and Catherine-Nicole Le Maure, yes." Voltaire nods, a gleam in his eye. "Two wonderful singers. Le Maure has the better voice, but I prefer Marie, simply because of her art. That woman can make you cry at the drop of a hat. I'm a great fan of both, as you say these days."

Things I didn't know. Once again, I'm amazed at the rich social life these ghosts lead. If anything, the opera community is proof life doesn't stop when you die. Not when it comes to experiencing all the beauty this world has to offer.

However, there's one thing I've found in my research that didn't quite make sense to me. "I've compared the dates between the building of the opera house and the sopranos' lifetimes." It was a very interesting read. The two had an epic rivalry. Neither killed anyone, but one came out of retirement to snatch up a role before it went to the other, and the other once went to prison for deliberately bombing a performance. Together they whipped up patrons into a frenzy worse than modern shipping wars. The Mauriens and the Pélissiens would've gone to bat hard for their favourite divas.

"Well, the dates don't add up. Charles Garnier is much younger than both of them. They were long dead by the time Napoleon III commissioned a new opera house. They never played there, only at Salle Le Peletier before it burnt down. So how come they're in the Palais Garnier now?"

"Ah." Victor folds his hands behind his back, ready to lecture me. "Well, it's more the idea of the Opéra national de Paris. Since it was first conceived in the 17th century, it's gone through many changes and many buildings, culminating in the Palais Garnier. And even that's changing. Nowadays, the Palais Garnier mainly stages ballet and a few classical operas, while the big shows have moved to the Opéra Bastille. Perhaps in a few decades the ghosts will move there, but for now, when people think of the Paris Opera, they think of the Garnier. And so, all the ghosts of musical history flock there. Those whose original buildings were destroyed even more so than others. It's a place of power in itself, a pillar of French culture."

A place of power. It's been a while since I've thought about those mystical places the Chevalier was obsessed with. To be honest, I haven't thought much about the Chevalier, either. I'm not surprised he hasn't tried to contact me after what happened at the Monastery of the Bears. Taking me in was about the worst decision he could've made. Several of his people were arrested because of me. He might've been arrested too. I shudder to think what they did to him once they'd found out who he was.

In the end, my dream of joining the Résistance was short-lived, much like the June Revolution Victor dramatised. At least those students lasted three days. I didn't even last the night.

"Alix? Are you still with us?" Victor asks kindly.

I blink, surprised to find tears in my eyes. The truth is, I still have nightmares about it. Not every night, but when I do, I find it impossible to fall asleep again. The sudden light, the frantic flight, the panic, Sébastien's iron grip. I know he went with them to protect me, but the memory reminds me he's still a GoPol officer. He may be testing the waters of going rogue, but as far as I know, he hasn't exactly jumped in yet.

"Sorry. It just triggered something."

Without another question, Victor pulls me into a hug. "You're doing great, kid. I'm proud of you. Keep your head above the water, okay?"

I take a deep breath, shaking off the last remnants of my bad memories. "So, this presence. Do you know anything about it?"

I look into everyone's faces expectantly, but they all shake their heads.

"Probably not a ghost," Voltaire muses. "A ghost would never dare desecrate the stage like that."

"Are you thinking of helping Monsieur Garnier?" Victor asks, a hint of concern in his voice.

"I'll have a look around, nothing more. I have a friend who works there who can get me backstage, and Sébastien has agreed to investigate."

Before I can promise Victor I'll be careful, Voltaire declares, "I think I will join your endeavour."

"You will?" None of the ghosts have ever offered to help before. It's always been a *me* thing, something for the living to deal with.

"Of course. It's been far too long since I've been to the opera. At least a decade or two. It's high time I made myself known again."

Oh, I see. This is more about promenading around and blessing all the performers with his presence. Still, I appreciate the gesture. We've truly come a long way.

"I'd love to have you there."

CHAPTER 13

O
n Monday I return to the Palais Garnier during the day. Théo's working in the archive today. We texted earlier so he knows I'm coming. I'm well aware how awkward it is, but he's come to terms with it and seems quite happy to show me around when his duties allow.

The opera's still open. Despite the scandal, posters are up, announcing the next performance. It turns out the performance of Medée was the penultimate of its run. They cancelled the last performance out of respect, but now they're ready to continue with their schedule. There was a winter ballet last weekend and they're already advertising a short run of Castor et Pollux. Although I know who Castor and Pollux were, I didn't know there was an opera about them until I'd read up on the divas. Apparently, Marie Pélissier originated the role of Telaira, the female lead.

While waiting for Théo to meet me in the foyer, I read the brief programme and familiarise myself with the opera. Both twins, one immortal, the other mortal, fell in love with the same woman, Telaira. But while trying to win her hand, Castor was slain. Realising he could never win Telaira's heart, Pollux made a deal with Jupiter to trade places with his dead brother. But his brother wouldn't accept the sacrifice and only returns for a single day to say goodbye—and to drive the second female character to suicide when she mistakes him for his brother. After everything descends into a great royal mess, Jupiter allows the twins to share immortality and throws them into the sky, where their constellation rises and falls every year. I should know, I'm a Gemini.

"Mademoiselle Dubois!" There's Garnier, sounding positively excited. "You decided to help."

As before, I ignore him. Today I have to be extra careful. Théo can get me behind closed doors, but that doesn't mean it's safe. Especially since he always seems to notice when I talk to ghosts. He's decided I'm a weirdo and dismissed it, and it's better if we keep it that way.

"They arrested the wrong person last night. Can you imagine? Meanwhile, we almost had a fire in the costume room. One of ours noticed it and we managed to alert one of the—"

"Alix!"

Thank god Théo's here. I want to know who's been arrested, but I can't ask Garnier. Maybe I can get that info from Théo later. For now, I'm glad he's saved me from giving in to my curiosity.

We kiss on the cheek, and he leads the way through one of the back doors. "Did you know they originally had a stable as part of the opera house?" he asks as we cross a large hall. "The carriages would drop people off right here in this foyer, so they didn't have to get their feet dirty in bad weather. Pretty cool, right?"

"Very." Especially since I witness a ghostly carriage pulling up and two groomsmen attending to it, while an elderly couple in splendid period dress exit.

"How long have you been working here?" I hope it sounds conversational.

Théo opens a door and leads me into a long corridor with many doors. Pieces of scenery and boxes lean against the wall, making the corridor something of an obstacle course. Especially as I have to skilfully avoid the many ghosts without attracting Théo's attention. "I used to help out with odd jobs here and there when my brother got the position. They didn't have any vacancies, but after about four months something miraculously popped up." He gives me a wry grin. "Laurent basically found a job for me."

"They created the position for you?"

"Yep. I mean, he put in a pretty savvy proposal. Someone *should* digitise the archive and the archivist didn't have time for it, so here

I am. This was about, well, two years ago. When I started at the Sorbonne."

Of course I remember. Théo joined our class in second year after moving from Lyon. There was a spark between us then, but I never got to act on it before he decided I wasn't worth pursuing. Probably because I ignored him in favour of Victor. I mean, who wouldn't? Théo is competent and smart, but he's no Victor Hugo.

Besides, he's had it in for me ever since. I, for one, haven't forgotten our debates about the catacombs. For the sake of the ghosts, I'm willing to play nice. There's a certain irony in the fact that the guy who fought against their rights is now assisting me to help them.

"So, you moved in with your brother?" I realise how little I know about my infuriating classmate.

He gives me a long look, as if weighing up how much he's willing to share. "We're pretty close. And I get to live with him," he adds, grinning at me. "Speak of the devil"—a door opens in front of us and a man in his early thirties steps out—"Laurent!"

Laurent looks exactly like his brother, if you add a decade. When he smiles at us, I'm reminded of those first glances I shared with Théo. They both have the same sweet smile. "Théo. And who's this young lady?"

"Alix, this is my brother Laurent," Théo introduces me before shrugging his shoulders. "This is Alix."

A surprised "oh" slips through Laurent's lips and his smile widens into a grin. Then he joins us, and we kiss cheeks. "It's an honour to finally meet you, Alix."

Confused, I look back and forth between him and Théo. "Finally?"

"See, little Théo here told me—" Laurent doesn't get very far before Théo rams his elbow into his belly. "Ouch, not my diaphragm. I need that." He smiles at me. "I'm playing Pollux this weekend. You should come," he adds with a sideways glance at his brother. "I can get you tickets."

"She's got a boyfriend," Théo informs him.

"You didn't tell me." Laurent looks at me apologetically. "Two tickets then?"

Slowly, my mind connects the dots. Laurent is rooting for Théo and me. He's just a bit behind the times. "It's all quite new, but sure, the show sounds great." It gives me an excuse to come back.

We walk down the corridor together. Apparently, Laurent is now part of our tour. "Honestly, I hope we make it in time. You must've heard what happened?"

"Alix was there," Théo interjects. "In the audience."

"Oh, shit." Laurent frowns. "Sorry about that."

"It's not like you planned the murder."

For a moment Laurent's face freezes, then he laughs as the words sink in. "No, no, we didn't. It's a shame, really, and it screws up the new show. You know, Ems was supposed to play Telaira, and now we have to redo the whole thing with Alexandra. Guess she got what she wanted after all," he adds, a little miffed.

"She wanted this?" I couldn't help noticing how Laurent seemed to panic for a moment when I suggested he'd *planned* the murder. Hopefully just a misunderstanding or frayed nerves. I've already spoken to too many murderers in my life.

"Not the murder, of course, but the role, you know." Laurent shakes his head and grimaces. "Alexandra is a pain to work with. She's so entitled. It's as if she's the only star and we 'youngsters' are all beneath her. Dreadful woman. Honestly, I wouldn't be surprised if *she's* the one behind this, instead of sweet old Madame Pirot."

"Who's that?"

Laurent smiles affectionately. "Our head costumer. They took her in because she was the last person to work on the dress, but she loved Ems. Everybody did."

"Everyone except Alexandra," Théo points out.

It seems to me everyone at the opera is as anxious to find out about this as I am. At least it won't seem strange for me to ask questions along those lines now. "You think she did it?"

Laurent takes a deep breath and puffs up his cheeks before answering, "Let's put it this way: I wouldn't put it past her. She threw a massive tantrum when they decided on the roles for Castor et Pollux. Too bad nobody filmed it or it would've gone viral." He shudders. "She terrorised Ems. Petty things like trampling the flowers in her dressing room. Hiding her shoes. She was never caught, but we all knew she was behind it." He nods back towards the door he came out of. "I told the police, but they warned me about slander. 'Just the facts, please'," Laurent says in a silly voice. "These are the facts."

Théo gives me a look behind Laurent's back, as if to apologise on his brother's behalf.

"Were you and Em...anuelle close?" I ask kindly, instead.

He rubs his neck ruefully. "It was nothing."

"They ended up in bed together after the Medée opening party." You can always count on younger siblings to rat you out.

"It was a one-off. We're friends. *Were* friends," he adds sadly, before admitting, "Maybe I had a little crush. We bonded over our families." Théo clears his throat, but his brother continues. "We both have younger siblings we basically took care of."

"Natalie, right? Her sister?"

Laurent looks at me in surprise. "You know her?"

"She was our usher that weekend."

"Poor thing. The two of them have had a rough time, but they've become very close over the last few years." He suddenly puts an arm around Théo's shoulders and pulls him in. "Just like us."

"Let go!" Théo grunts before he manages to escape the wrestling grip. "It's not the same."

"What is?" I ask curiously. Technically, it's none of my business, but Laurent seems so nice, and I like seeing Théo like this. He seems more himself than he does at university, where he hides in his pack of bros.

Théo moans. "Laurent, please." When his brother raises an eyebrow, Théo sighs. "Fine. Our parents died when I was eleven. Car accident. Laurent was only twenty-two and had already moved out. He was about to graduate from the CNSMD and had already booked an engagement out of town, but he put it all on hold to take me in instead."

"Oh, come on, you make it sound like I gave up my dreams. I just took a little break."

"You worked in a supermarket."

Laurent shrugs. "I already did that to pay for my studies. And I continued my vocal lessons. It all worked out in the end. I managed to keep you alive, and I got this job." He tries to ruffle Théo's hair, but the younger man narrowly avoids the gesture. "That's what you do for the family, isn't it?"

No way, he's the killer. Laurent is like the older brother I've always wanted but never had. Instead, I got Hélène. "My older sister threw me out of the car in the pouring rain."

Both brothers turn to me in horror. "Why?" Théo asks.

Why did I say that? It's not like I can explain the whole dilemma to them. Instead, I try to wave them off. "We're going through a bit of a rough patch, that's all," I say, using the words Laurent used to describe Natalie and Emanuelle's relationship. To lighten the mood, I add: "It's okay, I've still got a younger sister and we're cool. We don't need the older one."

"Three girls, huh?" Laurent chuckles. "Bet that was a lively household."

I laugh. "Just ask my parents."

"I didn't know you had two sisters," Théo says, sounding as if he had a right to know.

"Well, I didn't know you had a brother, either," I reply. "Or anything, really."

Laurent's eyes narrow at Théo. "Yeah, what's up with that? I thought you li—"

"Shut up," Théo says, half-closing his eyes in frustration. "Just shut up."

His brother laughs and opens a door for us, revealing a narrow staircase. After Théo's gone through, he whispers to me, "No sooner had we moved here than he told me all about this girl called Alix."

"Laurent!" Théo shouts in horror. "That was two years ago!"

I keep my head down and climb the stairs to escape the embarrassment. It's just brotherly teasing, I tell myself. Odile would do the same, although she's the younger of us. The thing between Théo and me died a long time ago, and it's one ghost I'm definitely going to leave in peace.

Théo hurries up behind me. "I'm so sorry, Alix. Please ignore my brother. He doesn't know what he's talking about. I mean, yes, I had a crush on you back then, but it's over now, I promise."

"Yeah, he only talks about you once a week or so," Laurent interjects.

"I was complain—" Théo hisses before thinking better of it. "I told him about our discussions. Not exactly romantic stuff, is it?"

"He admires your intellect," Laurent whistles from below.

I don't know whether to laugh or cry. "Didn't I say I already had a boyfriend?"

"You did," Théo says, before hissing down, "She did."

"Who is it?" Laurent asks.

Judging by the look on Théo's face, he wants to know, too. Fortunately, that's the good thing about my fake relationship with Sébastien. Unlike Gaspar, it's visible to everyone. The thought leaves a bitter taste in my mouth. I was in a good, stable, loving relationship all December and Théo never batted an eye. But the moment he sees me being picked up by Sébastien, suddenly I'm normal enough for him.

"You'll meet him if these tickets aren't just a joke."

Laurent laughs. "Oh, you're on. But first, the best seats in the house."

I don't know what I expected after climbing those stairs for so long, but when I reach the top door, I find a maze of narrow bridges, cables, and beams. And no floor.

CHAPTER 14

F unny thing is, I can crawl through tiny, body-crushing spaces or cross underground lakes, but put me high above the ground and I suddenly don't feel so good. I wouldn't say I'm afraid of heights so much as I respect them. And this, high above the stage, demands every ounce of my respect.

"You don't have to do this," Théo says quietly, his hand brushing mine as if he thought about taking it but decided not to cross the line. "I can take you on a tour of the archives."

The archives sound fantastic at the moment, but before I can give in and beg to be taken back downstairs, I notice movement on the stage. A group of performers rush out and quickly take their places in full costume. Unlike what I saw last time, there's no fighter jet, no baggy jeans, no baseball bat instead of a sword. No, these costumes are sumptuous and opulent, perfectly in keeping with the period they're supposed to represent.

This is a ghost rehearsal, and there's no way I'm going to miss it.

"Is it safe?" I ask Théo.

"Yes. Just hold onto the railing. Like this." He steps out onto one of the narrow bridges, grabs the railing, and holds out a hand.

At first, I try to make it on my own, but when the metal vibrates under my feet, I take his hand all too readily. We walk slowly out onto the bridge until we're directly above the stage.

"Sit down," Théo says gently, showing me how to do so relatively safely.

Our legs are dangling from the bridge, and I hold on to the side rail for dear life. If it wasn't for Théo sitting next to me, I would've crawled back to the entrance. After a few deep breaths, I notice Laurent is sitting a few metres away from us, watching the stage with a small smile on his lips.

I turn my eyes to the stage as well, absorbing the ghosts below me. They're still setting up. One of the women starts singing, quickly followed by another. It takes me a moment to realise, but their exercises are contradictory, designed to show the other up—and annoy the hell out of everyone else.

These must be the divas: Marie Pélissier and Catherine-Nicole Le Maure. Both are magnificent, but I wish I could hear them one at a time.

"This is my favourite place," Théo says, drawing my attention away from the ghosts. "High above this little world. It's where I can think best."

Downstairs, the divas have a go at each other, claiming the space for themselves. The director's trying to keep the piece together, but the other performers are quickly forming teams. I don't know how Théo can think with all that screaming and high-pitched singing, because I'm far too involved in the drama below.

"It's *my* role," says the stout little woman in the pretty grey wig. "I created the role. It has always been mine." Her words make me suspect she's Marie Pélissier.

That makes the taller, slimmer woman Catherine-Nicole Le Maure. She huffs. "I think it's high time we changed direction. We must not bore the public. Besides, the arias suit me much better." Her followers are quick to agree, and the Pélissiens are infuriated.

"Arias, arias. The people want emotion," says one man. "They want a Telaira that's broken and devastated, whose heart belongs to Castor, even though he's long dead."

As if on cue, Marie falls to the floor in pure heartbreak. The aria bursts from her lips, hauntingly beautiful. She hits all the notes but lets her voice break in just the right places to convey the tears she's crying. It almost makes me want to cry with her.

"You're always somewhere else," says Théo.

Startled, I look at him. "What?" I feel something wet on my cheek and quickly turn away, hoping he hasn't seen it. Suddenly, I miss Gaspar so much. I may not be his twin brother, but I would go to the underworld in a heartbeat for him if it'd bring him back.

Théo sighs. "I said you're always somewhere else, in your own world. You never see..." He brushes it off and leans forward on the bar, eyes cast down as if he sees something other than an empty stage.

Shit. I was watching the ghosts and he noticed. How do I save this? I clear my throat nervously. "Sorry, I'm just trying not to freak out."

He lifts his chin again. "Oh, I'm sorry. Come on, let's go back." He stands immediately and offers me his hand again.

I wish I could stay and watch more of the ghosts, especially now that Le Maure is singing, and boy, does her voice soar. I understand why Voltaire prefers her singing, despite being a huge fan of Pélissier. Unfortunately, I can't afford to make another mistake. Who knows who else Théo is talking to about me?

His brother looks surprised when we get up. "Back already? I thought you two—"

"What?" Théo snaps. "Were going to cuddle? Kiss on the beams?" He sounds positively annoyed. "That's not going to happen."

I can no longer ignore what Théo has only hinted at. Humiliated, I let go of his hand and make my way to the exit, muttering, "That ship sailed years ago."

"Alix!" Théo calls after me, while some of the ghosts below shout at us to be quiet.

Just then, a beautiful piece of music reaches my ears. What makes it so special is that it's not an aria, it's not even a classical piece. Muffled in the walls, I pick up a beat that makes my heart race and reminds me of a night danced away underground. Of sweet kisses in the early hours of morning.

"Where's that coming from?" Théo asks. While I was standing there, rooted to the spot, he's caught up with me. "Do you hear that?"

I swallow as I realise the music is real and not the memory of a ghost. "Probably just someone playing their phone."

"There's nobody up here. Except us," Théo argues. "We're literally under the roof."

"Then it must be the Angel of Music," Laurent jokes from behind us. "It wouldn't be the first time someone's heard music in the walls."

To my dismay, the music's faded. All that's left are the divas singing below, now harmonising in a peculiar way. I swallow hard and blink. "The Angel of Music?" It's as if I'm only now remembering why I'm here in the first place. "You mean the Phantom exists?"

Théo shakes his head. "The Phantom is just an invention. It always was."

"Oh, don't say that too loudly." Laurent chuckles. "Some people here swear they've seen or heard it. Even Ems initially thought it was the Phantom coming after her, but there never was a Phantom. I promise."

"There is one now," a voice whispers near my left ear. It's the same voice as in the box.

I whirl around and would've lost my balance if not for Théo's arms. "Careful."

"Watch out!" Laurent shouts suddenly.

Not a fraction of a second later, a broken cable whizzes past, missing Théo's ear by a millimetre. His face turns white as a sheet, and suddenly he's the one fighting for his balance. Luckily, Laurent is there to steady his brother before he falls to his death on the stage.

The cable swings back, but it's lost most of its force and just smacks into the railing, making the metal beneath my feet vibrate. I'm off the bridge in a flash, clinging to the apparent safety of the doorframe as if my life depended on it.

Below, the ghosts have stopped rehearsing. Instead, they're staring and pointing at us, and I can hear at least one saying, "The Phantom's back."

Laurent leads Théo to safety and shoos us into the stairwell. He looks almost as shocked as his brother. "This has never happened before. Alix, I'm so sorry. Théo, are you okay?"

Théo gasps for air. He nods. "I'm fine. I just... Gosh, that was scary." Still in shock, he wipes his cheek and finds blood on his fingers. Apparently, the cable *did* hit him after all. "Was that...?" He looks at his brother. "It was an accident, right?"

For a moment, Laurent says nothing. Then he puts his hand on Théo's shoulder and smiles. "Of course it was." But when his eyes meet mine, the message is a different one.

I think the killer might still be in the building.

CHAPTER 15

We make our way back down in uncomfortable silence. Did someone really just try to kill Théo or was it a freak accident? Apart from working in the same place, he has no connection with Emanuelle. Unless the cable was meant for Laurent. I suppose it's pretty hard to direct a cable once it's been cut. The killer could've got the timing or the direction wrong. After all, Laurent was close to Emanuelle and he made no secret of his dislike for the diva of the house.

I've seen Alexandra Briot as Medée. She's a singer in her mid-forties with a long list of accolades, and she carries herself as if she were one of the stars of the silent film era. Of course, that may have been just her role, but somehow I can't imagine the plump woman hiding in the rafters in case Laurent was there. On the other hand, Théo said it was his favourite place. It seems to be something of a secret spot for the brothers, a safe haven away from the chaos of their lives.

Maybe it wasn't Alexandra herself, but one of her followers. I've only seen ten minutes of Pélissier and Le Maure and I'm ready to believe their fans would kill for them if they weren't already all dead.

A door opens in front of us, and I see a familiar face step out. Her eyes are red and her cheeks flushed.

"Natalie," Laurent calls. He pushes past Théo and me and hurries to her side. "How are you?"

As he comforts the young usher, Théo whispers, "That was Emanuelle's dressing room. She was probably crying in there."

I cluck my tongue. "Of course she was. How would you feel if your brother was murdered?"

Théo straightens up and swallows hard. "Bloody awful. He's all I've got."

Great. Now I feel sorry for Théo. How terrible it must've been for him to lose both his parents so suddenly and so young. I'm glad his older brother stepped up and took care of him, even if he had to put his own dreams on hold for a while. Everyone should have at least one person who'll go to the ends of the earth for them. I have Gaby and he has Laurent.

"Thank you for showing me around today." And for showing me a bit of the real Théo.

He raises his eyebrows. "You're leaving already?"

"I don't think it's the right time. Everyone here's in mourning for Emanuelle and I'm the intruder."

"We could hide in the archives."

"And do what? Cuddle? Kiss?" I echo his earlier indignation. No, the last thing I want is to be alone with Théo after learning he still has a crush on me.

Théo lowers his head. "I'm sorry." He rubs his neck. "Laurent gets in my head sometimes. He thinks we should be together, but to be honest, I can't imagine it." I bet he's never told his brother how weird I am. "And you're obviously not interested in me. I mean, you have a boyfriend, don't you?" He smiles, but it's not very convincing. "Sorry, I'm making this awkward."

Oh, yes. "I *do* have a boyfriend. You know what the best thing about him is? He doesn't judge me for my quirks." That's true whether I'm talking about Gaspar or Sébastien.

I leave Théo there, say a quick goodbye to Laurent, and head back to the entrance. The truth is I wish I had more time at the opera. I've learnt a lot about Théo and his brother, but I haven't found out anything about this menacing presence. The cable was an accident, I decide, and the only interesting thing I saw was the ghost rehearsal. Unfortunately, I can't think of a way to carry out my investigation with Théo or his wingman of a brother breathing down my neck.

So, I leave the opera without much more information than Laurent's gossip. If Alexandra really is behind all this, I'm sure the police will find out. They don't need me to investigate the murder.

Despite the rain, I take a deep breath outside. All this drama in one place is exhausting.

I'm walking away from the opera when a car pulls up next to me. My heart skips a beat, but then I recognise the car and my sister inside. Hélène looks at me with a deep frown. "What are you doing here?"

"None of your business." I keep walking, while she keeps pulling the car along.

"Get in. I'm on my way home, anyway."

I stop and give her a long look. "Why would I do that? So you can kick me out again?"

"Don't be ridiculous, Alix. I need to talk to you."

For a moment I consider ignoring her. The last time I was in the car it was a disaster. We said things to each other that weren't very sisterly, but then I think of Théo and his brother and Natalie and her dead sister. "Fine." I open the door and get in just as someone honks.

Hélène waits until I've fastened my seatbelt before pulling away from the curb. "For what it's worth, I'm sorry I threw you out in the rain. That wasn't very mature of me."

Look at that, an apology. She probably expects me to recipro-cate, but I'm still too hurt about what she and Cédric did to me.

"But you said some terrible things," she quickly follows her apology with some accusations of her own.

Here we go. "So did you."

Hélène takes a few deep breaths as we wait for the light to change. "Well, I'm glad you're doing better."

"What do you mean?" I'm absolutely miserable.

"You've got a new boyfriend, haven't you?"

"Oh yeah, everything's better now that I have a living, breathing boyfriend." At least I don't have to pretend Gaspar doesn't exist in front of her.

She gives me a quick glare, clearly annoyed. "Come on. You have to agree it's much better this way. At least he's someone you can bring to the wedding. It'll make Cédric happy," she adds with an eye-roll.

Cautiously, I probe her further: "You don't sound happy.

"Well, while I appreciate that you've given up all this ghost nonsense and found yourself a real boyfriend, he's not exactly a catch, is he?"

"Um, what?" In what world would Sébastien not be a catch. "Have you seen him?"

Hélène waves me off with her hand. "Sure, sure, he's hot, but he's a bit of an ass, don't you think? Thinks he's too good for his family. Cédric told me how they never got along as kids. Not because Cédric didn't try."

"Of course." A familiar anger bubbles up inside me.

"It's true. Cédric held out his hand for years and all Sébastien did was spit on it."

"Because Cédric was just trying to use him. Cozying up to his cousin to get into GoPol".

Hélène scoffs and and almost crashes into the car in front of us as it comes to a halt. She honks and curses at the other driver before driving past. "'Cozying up to your cousin'," she imitates. "As if that's a bad thing. They're cousins, for god's sake. It's only natural he wants them to be close." She takes a deep breath and continues, "Cédric wanted to be there for him. When his mother left, you know." She looks at me, as if to see if I actually know this.

"You can hardly blame someone for their mother leaving."

She clicks her tongue. "Of course not, but he could've had Cédric at his side. Cédric would have been there for him. Instead, that little prick bit the hand that fed him."

"Wow. Is that what Cédric calls him? Little prick?"

"That's what *I* call him. Cédric is much too nice. He says it's forgotten and forgiven. They're working together now, and he wants to make the best of it." She gives me a worried look. "He's not a good man, Alix."

I almost laugh at her face. Of all the Roubert men—or Villeneuf, in Cédric's case—Sébastien is by far the best. Except for Dix, but he's basically the same person, just a little less broken.

"Why don't *you* get me a boyfriend, Léni?" I say in a sickly sweet voice. "Since you don't like Gaspar or Séb."

"With that track record, maybe I should."

"Let me out."

"We're almost home," Hélène snaps, then sighs. "Look, I'm just trying to look after you. That's what big sisters do."

I wonder if Laurent ever told Théo how to live his life. Judging by how supportive he seemed, I can't imagine it.

For a moment I'm too angry to speak. We pull into our street and Hélène is lucky enough to find a parking space right in front of our house.

Grateful for the nearby shelter, I get out the car. But when I see her stupid face across the roof, I can't keep it in. "If you really cared about me, you'd get rid of the scum who betrayed me."

Hélène pales. "What did you just say?"

"You heard me. Sébastien is not the bad apple in the family. Your fiancé is." Or rather, Sébastien is the only good apple in the family. "He used Séb like he used me. And he'll use you if it suits his ambitions. If you cared at all about me, or even yourself, you'd call off the wedding and kick that disgusting pile of shit to the curb," my voice shakes at the harsh words. Tears well up in my eyes as I remember the horror of the sting operation, the shock of Cédric's betrayal.

"That's it," Hélène's voice is just as shaky as she circles the car and stomps on the pavement. "You're out. I've tried, Alix. I've really, really tried to be a good sister to you, but you're hell-bent on ruining your life, and I refuse to be dragged down by you. You're out. Out of my wedding. Out of my life."

"I didn't want to go to your stupid wedding anyway," I shout back. "Have fun being Madame Scumbag!"

As I turn to leave, Hélène shouts at me, "Where are you going? You live up there."

So much for her life. "I'm going to sleep at Sébastien's. Somewhere where I don't have to see you."

"Fine! Run away from the real world. That's what you've always done."

Right now, all I want to do is run away from the mean woman who calls herself my sister.

CHAPTER 16

No one is more surprised than I when I actually turn up at Sébastien's door. I only said that to spite Hélène and keep up my ruse. I could've easily gone to Gaby's, instead. I *should've* gone to Gaby's, instead. And yet here I am, a little wet from the rain, ringing the doorbell off the wall, not knowing if he's even home.

A buzzing sound alerts me to the door unlocking. I push it open and step into the dark corridor. I can still turn around, but I'm wet and cold, and I really need a friend right now.

My feet carry me upstairs. Sébastien opens the door to his apartment before I have a chance to ring the bell. His face is glistening with sweat and he's wearing a tight black shirt that shows off every line of his well-toned muscles. "It's you," he says in surprise. He lifts his shirt to wipe his face, giving me a glimpse of his six-pack.

I don't know who he expected to see looking like that. "Can I come in?"

He opens the door wider. "Of course. Are you alright?" His worried gaze scans my face like it's a puzzle to be solved. Can he see I've been crying?

"Look," I begin, "I just need a place to crash for a bit." I notice the door to the right is open and catch a glimpse of some exercise equipment. That explains the sweat.

"You want to sleep here?"

Shit! Why did I say that? There's no way we're at that stage in our relationship. Gosh, we don't even have a relationship. "I'm sorry. I should go."

But when I turn around, he grabs my wrist and pulls me into his apartment. "Of course you can stay." The door closes behind me. "What happened?"

I try to speak, but there's this huge frog in my throat. All that comes out is a muffled hiccup.

Sébastien puts his hand on the small of my back. "Would you like some coffee? Or some wine? Or do you want to take a shower? I'll just need to grab a tow—"

The doorbell rings again.

"Shoot! That's my father."

Alarmed, I look up at him. His father's here? "I thought this was a safe place. Sorry, I should go."

"Don't. Besides, you don't want to meet him on the stairs." Sébastien presses the buzzer for the downstairs door before opening the door to his left. His bedroom. "You can stay in here. I'll make it quick."

He gives me a gentle nudge and closes the door behind him.

My heart pounds in my chest. The last time I was face to face with Charles, he practically threatened to get rid of me. And I believed him. From what I know of him, it was no idle threat.

The doorbell rings again and I hear Sébastien open the door. In a panic, I hurry away from the wall behind me and sit on his bed, my fingers digging into the bedspread. Sébastien's bedroom is as sparsely furnished as his living room. My heart eases a little when I see another row of greenery in front of the window. Otherwise, there's not much to see. There's a wardrobe and a chair with some dirty clothes on it. And there's the bed, big enough for company if needed. He's also got candles spread around the room, and I wonder if he gets romantic visitors often.

I run a hand through my wet hair and sigh. Hiding in his bedroom wasn't part of the plan. I really shouldn't be here. Then again, he's seen mine.

"Where is he?" Charles' voice makes my adrenaline surge again. For a moment I'm afraid he's looking for me, but then the pronoun sinks in. It's Dix he wants. "If you know where he is—"

Sébastien's voice is softer, calmer, as he interrupts his father, and I hear the two of them moving into the living room.

Part of me is still scared shitless, while another part wants to listen in. To stop myself from doing something stupid, I pull out my mobile instead. It's high time I spoke to Gaby.

Hélène uninvited me from her wedding today, I write, *we had a big fight. Again.*

It doesn't take long for her to write back. *Are you okay?*

I'm at Séb's, but his father just arrived.

Alix! Do you need a getaway car?

I smile, remembering how quickly she and Marie organised one at the New Year's Eve party. *No, it's alright. He won't be staying long. Got to keep up the act, you know?*

"Well, what have you done to rectify the situation?" shouts Charles suddenly. "It's been eight weeks! Your stupid whisper ghost has been on the run for eight weeks." His voice grows louder and louder.

In contrast, Sébastien keeps his voice down. To no avail.

"Whatever you're doing, it's not working! Get a grip, son! Until you've sorted this out, you're off duty. I don't need a defective whisperer."

"I'm not defective." I guess even Sébastien has his limits.

The vibration in my hand reminds me I've been texting Gaby. She's already on her fourth message.

I really don't know why you're doing this to yourself. There must be another way.

You don't have to stay in a toxic situation. I can come and get you. And if that asshole has a problem with that, he'll answer to me.

The last thing I want is for Charles to know Gaby.

Just say the word and I'll be there.

Alix?!

Just as I'm about to reply, I feel a knot in my stomach. Someone else is in the room. And as the door is still very much closed, that someone is a ghost.

I stare at my phone, where another message is coming in, but I can't even see it. Instead, I listen intently for the other presence in the room. *Please let it be Dix.* Even though it'd be terrible timing with Charles in the other room, I really hope it's him. But I don't dare turn around, don't dare acknowledge it.

The phone. Gaby needs an answer and I need to do something.

Alix, please! My friend has written. *I need you to answer me.*

I'm fine, I answer.

"Well, well, well," a deep voice says, sending shivers of fear down my spine. It's not Dix. It's someone worse. Much, much worse. "Who have we got here?"

In a panic, I call Gaby. A moment later I remember to lift the phone to my mouth as well. "No, I'm telling you, it's not like that." At least my voice is working. "We didn't sleep together." I manage a shaky laugh and fall back on the bed for extra effect and a wider peripheral view.

C-Trente is right next to the bed, looking down at me.

131

"You didn't...?" Gaby asks confused, but luckily she's a smart cookie and catches on quickly. "Then what *did* you do?" Her voice sounds a little tense.

"We just cuddled in bed and talked. It was really nice."

"I know you can see me," C-Trente says in a threatening drawl. "You can't fool me."

"He even brought me breakfast in bed." I giggle, twirling a lock of hair between my fingers. "I know!" I say before Gaby has a chance to reply. "I didn't expect that either. He's so sweet."

Instead of playing along, Gaby whispers, "If there's someone in the room with you, tell me about the eggs."

"Well, he didn't get out the crêpes, just croissants and butter, some eggs. It wasn't too fancy, but everything tastes better when you're fed, right?"

C-Trente makes a retching sound. Out of the corner of my eye, I see him step through the wall into the living room.

"He'd better keep you safe, or I'll fry his eggs," Gaby says in a trembling voice.

There are footsteps in the hallway and my heart almost jumps out of my throat. "I hope so, too." Damn, that didn't sound as happy and excited as I'd hoped.

"You should've told me," I hear Charles shout from the door.

"You shouted at me," says Sébastien.

"She's—"

"My girlfriend," Sébastien reminds him. "Remember? Alix is my girlfriend. And I'd appreciate it if you didn't scare her off."

Something intense is going on outside the door and I feel like I'm about to faint.

"Alix?" Gaby's voice is like an anchor holding me to this world.

"I can't..." That's as far as I get with an explanation before my airways shut down. *Please don't come in here.*

There's footsteps in the corridor, then a door slams. But before I can breathe a sigh of relief, C-Trente enters the room. I stare through him at the door. Slowly he comes closer and fills my entire vision. My eyes itch. Any moment, I'll start to cry and then the gig is over.

Fortunately, Gaby is still on the phone. "Are you having eggs again? Please, Alix, please speak."

"I don't really feel like omelette tonight," I whisper. C-Trente is right in front of me, reaching for me. Panic seizes my chest. I can pretend not to see him all I want. If he touches me, it'll give me away as clearly as if I were talking to him.

"Get out!" Sébastien's voice is like the crack of a whip.

I blink, startled as I should be. "What?"

"Not you. Him," Sébastien snarls. "This is my flat. You're not allowed in here. So, get out."

"What the hell is going on over there?" Gaby asks. She must be picking up some of it over the phone.

C-Trente stares at me for a moment before slowly turning to Sébastien. "You're playing a dangerous game, boy. Are you sure it's just the idiot who's gone rogue?"

I finally see Sébastien as C-Trente moves aside. Despite being a few centimetres shorter than the imposing whisper ghost, he stares him down. "You're violating the code of conduct. Who's going rogue now?"

C-Trente sneers. "You'd be exceptionally stupid to risk it all for her. Don't think for a moment that you'd be safe from the consequences."

"One last time," Sébastien growls. "Get out!"

I don't dare watch as C-Trente leaves the room, never once looking away from Sébastien.

"What's going on?" Gaby asks on the verge of tears. "Alix, please!"

Even though he's gone, I can't breathe. I'm afraid he's just bluffing, biding his time until he can catch us unawares. Sébastien quickly crosses the room and lights three of the candles. Their fire gives off a strong smell of herbs. "Vervain, it repels ghosts."

I blink. On the phone, Gaby is losing her mind. "That's it, I'm coming to get you. I just need the address," she adds, realising the flaw in her plan.

Sébastien approaches me with a worried frown. "Alix?"

"It was near the Arc de Triomphe, wasn't it? I'll just go to every door and—"

Sébastien kneels down in front of me and takes the phone from my lifeless hand. "Gaby? I've got her now."

Then he takes me in his arms, one hand behind my back, the other on my head, and presses me against his chest. "I've got you now."

CHAPTER 17

For an endless time, Sébastien's arms are my whole world. His heartbeat fills my ears and I breathe when he breathes. With each breath, the crust of shock that's encased me breaks a little more open. As the pieces fall away, the fear is laid bare. Soon I start to shake. Then the hiccups come, and my breathing gets out of sync. But I'm moving, no longer frozen. The tears are good. The tears mean I'm still alive.

"He knows," I whisper. "He knows."

"No, he doesn't." Sébastien is still holding me. His lower arm moves up and down as he strokes my back. "He may suspect, but you passed the test. You did it. You held your own with him. I'm so proud of you."

It doesn't feel like I held my own. Another minute and I'd have crumbled, sealing my fate. "What will they do when they find out?"

"Search for Petite Alix to finish what they started."

"And if they don't find her?" My Panthéon ghosts would never let them have her.

Sébastien's silence is answer enough.

"He'll get rid of me," I say in his place. "Your father will kill me."

"No, he won't."

I pull away to look at him. "How can you say that? He killed *you!*" Surely he won't spare me when he couldn't even stop at his own son.

"This is different. He could easily get away with me. I mean, I consented, so... it's different." Sébastien blinks, stumbling over the word "consented". "You've got people who'll miss you. Gaby will probably break down his door herself if she even suspects foul play."

Although that sounds like my friend, I'm not half as convinced of my safety net as he is. "He's done it before."

Sébastien frowns. Slowly, he pulls away and settles on the floor against the bed next to me. "What do you mean?"

"I discovered the Chevalier's true identity." Bit by bit, I tell him everything I learned from the file I stole. The file that made me enemy number one. Or two, after Romain. "He almost killed him and then took out his whisper ghosts and put him in prison."

"I remember him," says Sébastien, sounding a little shocked. "His junior partner. They were close, until one day they weren't. I asked him once what happened to him and he told me that he

137

broke the rules and paid for it." He frowns heavily. "It was one of those lessons. If you break the rules, you pay."

Do I want to know how Sébastien had to pay? I decide I don't and lean against him. C-Trente's threat to him plays in my head. "Are you okay?"

Sébastien laughs softly. "Am I okay? We should be worrying about you right now."

I put a hand on his chest and look into his eyes. "Sébastien, please. I didn't hear much, but your father was shouting at you."

"He does it all the time." That does the opposite of reassuring me. "Look, I messed up."

"How?"

"This whole thing with you." He drops his eyes and takes a deep breath. "From a GoPol point of view, I didn't handle it properly. I should've brought you in sooner, pushed you harder to find out about Petite Alix. I cut you too much slack, my father said, so it's my fault."

Unimpressed, I snort. "It's *your* fault I became a royal pain in his ass?"

My comment makes him laugh and he looks up again. "Pretty much. If I'd dealt with you promptly instead of this soft approach—my father's words, not mine—you never would have gotten too big for your breeches—again, his words." He winces apologetically. "You caused quite a stir, you know? Stealing a ghost from GoPol and running away. Never happened before. Not in my time."

"I didn't get very far."

"You were betrayed," Sébastien confesses.

"You mean Cédric? Did you know he told my sister a little sob story about how he kept reaching out to you, but you scoffed at him? She thinks you're the worst, so don't expect an invitation to the wedding."

He laughs again and relaxes slightly. "Are you surprised? I wasn't planning on going anyway."

My heart softens. "That's what I told her. I'm not going either. I've been officially kicked out of the wedding party."

"Is that why you came here?"

I settle back into my position by his side and rest my head on his shoulder. "She doesn't want me as a witness anymore, and to be honest, it's a relief. Can you imagine me signing a document, essentially blessing their union? I want Cédric as far away from her as possible, but Léni doesn't see it that way. For her, he's got sunshine coming out of his ass."

Sébastien chuckles at the image.

"He's got her all twisted around. I don't recognise her anymore." With a sigh I add, "I bet she's saying the same about me."

Sébastien puts an arm around me and squeezes my shoulder. "Like you said, Cédric's twisted her mind. I can see how, from his point of view, I'm the bad guy."

"He threw your mother's disappearance in your face. That was extraordinarily cruel."

"Yes, but he was right, wasn't he? My maman left me. She knew what my father was like, and she left—without me. Because she knew it wasn't worth it. I'm not the kind of guy people want to be around. Cédric always had many friends. He didn't need me. And look how well he's doing, while I'm here questioning everything I believe in. My father was right, I *am* defective".

My heart goes out to him. He's had such a lonely childhood. I can't even begin to imagine what it must've been like, growing up without friends, without siblings, with nothing but a demanding father. No, not a demanding one, an abusive one. "He alienated you. Your father. He alienated you from everyone who could've been in your life, until you were completely isolated, with nothing to live for but this vocation of his. You're not defective just because he can no longer control you so easily".

Sébastien gives me such a desperate look my heart breaks for him. "I like working with ghosts," he says in a weak defence.

"You enjoyed working with Dix. But he's your weak spot, and now your father wants to get rid of him. To make sure you're really all alone."

"He would make me a new whisper ghost."

"You mean he's going to kill you a second time, hoping someone less combative will be easier to control?"

Sébastien turns his head away and slips out from under me. "Is that what you think?"

Confused, I ask, "I think what?"

He gets to his feet. "That I don't have any fight left in me? That I'm easy to control? Is that it? That all my good sides died with Dix?"

Slowly I stand up. In a way, it is what I said. Put like that, though, I'm horrified. "They didn't. You... you're still him. I mean, that boy, that beautiful, rebellious boy is still inside you."

Sébastien blinks. His lower lip trembles and he inhales sharply. He looks at me as if he's drowning. Then, abruptly, he lowers his eyes, swallows and turns away. "I can't do it. There must be a way to convince my father to keep Dix. I just have to find him first and prove myself. And I promise I'll get him off your back. He's a hard man, but he does what he does to keep this country safe. Individual lives don't mean much in the grand scheme of things. The mission always comes first."

"You're not really selling it to me." I understand where he's coming from. He's looked up to his father his whole life. And going against GoPol, no matter how wrong they are, is scary. I know that first hand. So, I can't really blame him for not wanting to turn his whole life upside down. The fighting spirit didn't die with Dix, but it's buried deep under layers and layers of guilt, duty, and most of all, abuse.

I decide to give him a break, at least for today. "Alright. Enough of that. What's the next step?"

He looks so grateful it hurts. "There's been a development in the opera murder. I promised to help you with it, but I think they've found the murderer."

"Madame Pirot?" I ask doubtfully.

Sébastien frowns in surprise. "How do you know? Did Garnier tell you? Did he come to see you again?"

"Confession time. I went to the opera today."

"Alone?"

Well, this is embarrassing. I guess I'm not used to having a partner. "A friend of mine from university happens to work there. His brother is one of the tenors. He invited me to go backstage, and we saw a ghost performance. I mean, I saw one. He doesn't know anything about the ghosts, and I didn't give myself away." Oh dear, I'm rambling. Why am I rambling? "Anyway, Laurent—his brother—told us about Madame Pirot. He doesn't think she's the murderer."

"They found her DNA on the dress."

"Of course. I mean, she handled it, right?"

"Alix..."

I take a deep breath. "Laurent thinks Alexandra Briot is behind this. She's got a motive. Does Madame Pirot have a motive?"

"It hasn't been established yet."

"Well, there's something else." I quickly tell him about the incident with the cable that almost killed Théo. "At the time, Madame Pirot was already in custody. We also heard music."

Sébastien doesn't look very impressed. "At the opera?"

Okay, I should've been more specific. "The wrong kind of music. EDM music." I swallow hard. "Gaspar's kind of music. It came from the walls."

His posture changes as he starts to take me seriously. "You think Gaspar is involved?"

"No, I... I don't know." It doesn't make sense. Why would Gaspar be at the opera, and why would he murder some random soprano? Besides, he's a ghost. He doesn't leave fingerprints, but he can't put poison on clothes, either. It's nothing but wishful thinking. I just miss him so much.

Sébastien's jaw tightens as he nods abruptly. "We'll look into it. No stone left unturned."

I love that he's fully on board even though Gaspar is nothing but a ghost. I'm sure he has some thoughts about our relationship, but he doesn't devalue my feelings. "Thank you."

CHAPTER 18

I didn't sleep at Sébastien's that night. Instead, he offers to drive me to Gaby's and together we zoom through the city on his bike. Gaby couldn't be happier to have me back in her arms, and I'm grateful for her, too. She pulls me into her one-room flat and points to the bed.

"As you can see, Marie is here, but make yourself at home. She kept me sane while you went radio silent."

Marie is kneeling on the bed, looking out the window. "He's got a motorbike! That's pretty cool."

"It's bad for the environment," Gaby says, pushing me relentlessly towards the bed.

The truth is, I'm a bit overwhelmed. Was Marie there when I called Gaby? Did Gaby tell her everything?

Marie smiles and pats the bed. "Get in. I'll do your nails."

I see a whole collection of paints on the bedside table. I slowly get into bed and look at my nails, noticing I haven't taken much care of them lately. "Do you think you can save them?"

"They're not that bad. Nothing a little colour won't fix. Do you have a preference?"

Meanwhile, Gaby throws a pizza box on the bed. "There's still two slices in there. But we can order more if you're hungry."

Being with these two is like a cup of hot cocoa. Within minutes, I feel the last stubborn hooks of anxiety dissolve. I'm fed, pampered, and accepted. Even though I've turned up so late and obviously interrupted their date, they're there for me. "Is it too daring to wear black?"

Gaby clearly thinks so, but Marie smiles warmly. "Like Gaspar? Did you know I did his nails? That guy was hopeless with a brush." She picks up a black bottle and I can't help but wonder if it's the same one he used.

"I miss him so much."

"I know, honey." Gaby wraps her arms around me and buries her chin in my shoulder. "I'm so sorry."

Marie takes my left hand and puts it on a small purple pillow. "Will Sébastien mind if you wear Gaspar's colour? Not that black is a colour, but he'd argue it is."

I share a look with Gaby, who gives me a subtle shrug. Immediately, I know she hasn't betrayed me. Even though she's freaked out, she didn't give away my secret. She's just the best.

With a sigh, I decide it's high time I returned the favour. If she trusts Marie, so should I. I just need to remind her to stay out of this. "He won't mind. This thing between us... it's just an act."

"Alix," Gaby whispers in surprise. "Are you sure?"

Curious, Marie looks at me. "Why would you pretend to be with Sébastien?"

"To fool his father, his stupid cousin, and my sister." Probably a whole lot of other people, too, but I don't want to think about it. "The thing is... Petite Alix got away."

For a moment Marie is just confused. Then her eyes widen, and she gasps. "You can still see ghosts."

I nod. "I can, but I can't see Gaspar. He disappeared the day after I was captured. At first I thought I'd lost my powers, but then Sébastien came and brought me Petite Alix."

"He did?"

"Yes. It surprised me. Him, too, probably. I don't think he's ever done anything so daring." C-Trente was right. Sébastien is going rogue. He just isn't quite there yet.

While Marie paints my nails black like Gaspar's, I tell her all about the plan I made with Sébastien and why it's so important no one knows about it. Then I tell Gaby what really happened in his bedroom this afternoon, and she hugs me even tighter.

"I was so scared for you. What a creep!"

"But Sébastien did well, didn't he?" Marie asked. "Gaby told me he looked after you."

For a moment I remember his steady heartbeat beneath my ear, the protective pressure of his arms and his calm, soothing voice whispering in my hair.

"You know?" Marie turns my finished hand over and points to one of the lines on my palm. "When I first saw this double love line, I thought it represented Gaspar's dual existence. But he only really has one, right? What if you're meant to love someone else? In addition to Gaspar, of course."

"In addition?" I raise an eyebrow. "Like, what, a ghostly three-some?"

Gaby grins close to my ear. "A throuple."

My cheeks start to burn just at the thought. "No, no, that's not happening. That's..." I look into Marie's grinning face and blush even more. "You're messing with me!"

Gaby lets go of me with a gasp. "You totally just thought about it."

"I didn't! How would that even work?" My mind has some very interesting ideas. "They don't even like each other."

Marie wiggles her eyebrows. "But you like them. Both of them."

"No, I don't. I mean, yes, Gaspar, but Sébastien and I are just friends. That's all."

"What if Gaspar doesn't come back?" Gaby asks, immediately killing the mood. "What if he's really gone?"

I shake my head stubbornly. "I refuse to give up on him. Speaking of which. Marie, do you know where he's buried?"

She perks up. "I do. Weren't you... no, of course you weren't at his funeral. You didn't even know he was dead when they buried him. It's in Montparnasse. I can take you there."

"Yes, please. I know I shouldn't hope, but he might be there. Or maybe someone's seen him. I just need to make sure."

Marie nods. "Alright. I have to work most of the week, but we could do it at the weekend."

My heart wants to go now, but my head knows better. "The weekend is fine." If he's really there, he'll still be there in five days.

CHAPTER 19

Théo's brother comes through with the tickets and so Sébastien and I are back at the opera on Friday night for the opening night of Castor et Pollux. To my surprise, we're sitting in exactly the same box as before. You'd think the boxes would be too valuable to give away to friends and family, but there's no doubt about it when I pick up the tickets from the box office.

Confused, I show them to Sébastien.

"Maybe he's your secret benefactor. Nothing but the best for his brother's crush." He grimaces in disapproval.

"I should've never told you." To make sure we're on the same page, I told Sébastien all about Théo and his brother. I just felt I had to come clean, which is idiotic because I didn't do anything, and it shouldn't matter to Sébastien whether my classmate has feelings for me or not. I blame Gaby and Marie for getting into my head.

Sébastien seems amused. "But you did."

"Oh, don't be so smug about it." It's getting easier to be around him, almost as if we're real friends. I feel like I see shades of Dix in him, which shouldn't surprise me, yet somehow does.

He offers me his arm and together we walk up the Grand Staircase to the upper floor. Even though it's opening night, the crowds aren't as big as they were for Medée. I see a lot of old couples, probably subscribers for decades, who don't want to miss meeting their fellow subscribers to cast their verdict on whether this performance is worth their annual subscription or not. Apart from them, there are a few tourists and a few art critics. If I had to guess, I'd say about two-thirds of the seats will be filled. Not exactly what you want for opening night.

As we approach our box, I see we've got the same usher as before. Unlike two weeks ago, there are deep shadows under her eyes. This woman shouldn't be working. I wonder if she ever took time off to mourn.

"Good evening," she greets us. "Another date, I see." There's even a small smile for us.

"Natalie, was it?"

She looks at our tickets and nods to the box behind her. "It's all yours."

I put a hand on Sébastien's back and give him a gentle nudge. "Why don't you go ahead?" He glances at me before giving me some space. "Are you okay?"

Natalie's eyes widen. "What do you mean?" she asks in a small, tight voice.

"You just lost your sister." When her frown deepens, I add: "I saw you with Laurent on Monday. His little brother is a friend of mine and I went to see him at work."

Her face relaxes again. "Oh. Now I remember. You were with Théo. I didn't recognise you out of your fancy dress."

"You were a bit preoccupied. Really, I'm so sorry about your sister. I have two sisters myself and I can't imagine what it would be like to lose one." In a way, I've lost Hélène, but she's still alive and kicking. Mostly kicking a big fuss, but kicking all the same.

"She took care of me, even when I didn't want her to."

"In a good way or in that totally condescending 'I know better than you' way?" Because according to Hélène, she's only looking out for me as well.

Natalie laughs so suddenly she scares herself. Mortified, she covers her mouth. "I shouldn't laugh."

"Yes, you should. I'm sure your sister would've wanted you to." An uninvited memory of Gaspar arises. I don't have to wonder what he would've wanted for me. Live my life. Move on. But that's impossible so long as I don't know what's become of him.

"You're right. Emanuelle would've liked this. She always wanted people to be happy and wouldn't give up until they were. I used to hate her so much when I was younger. It definitely felt like the latter you mentioned. She was the perfect one and I was the mess, but she really *was* perfect and she took care of me when everyone else wrote me off. I owe her my life."

"Again, I'm so sorry for your loss."

"Thank you."

If she weren't a complete stranger, I'd hug her. As it is, a smile will have to do.

With a heavy heart, I enter the box and take my seat next to Sébastien. As I'd thought, the tiers are only half full. A few people are still waiting to be seated, but it won't be a full house. For a moment, I'm under the impression I missed the beginning, since the orchestra is playing and a woman is singing. Then I see the curtains are still closed.

It's Le Maure and some ghostly musicians, gracing the opera with a pre-show event.

"Ah, what a voice," someone beside me says.

When I look up this time, I see a familiar figure in a fancy wig and royal blue waistcoat. "Voltaire!"

On the other side of me, Sébastien startles. He's been watching Le Maure, lost in thought, but now his eyes widen. "Vol... *the* Voltaire?"

Smug as ever, Voltaire gives him a sharp nod. "Indeed. And you must be the boy's whisperer. What was his name? Dix-Sept?" He wrinkles his nose at the soulless number given to all GoPol ghosts.

"You know Dix?" Sébastien asks, still clearly in awe.

"I met him once, when he agreed to help our Alix."

"Your Alix," Sébastien repeats, but swallows half the words.

Voltaire gives him one of his most withering stares. "I want you to know we will come after you if you ever think of harming her."

Sébastien stares at him a little longer. Then he breaks eye contact and chuckles softly. "This will never cease to amaze me."

"What?" He's not usually this flustered about ghosts.

His eyes meet mine. "How you got them to care about you."

"That's easy," Voltaire says. "She cared about us first."

The performance was amazing. It's a completely different experience when you know the lead actor personally. Laurent transformed on stage. He wasn't the goofy older brother, but the battle-hardened soldier, hopelessly in love with Telaira, and heartbroken over his dead twin brother. The brotherly bond is the heart of the story. And while I feel a little sorry for Telaira for losing her beloved, and even more for the other female lead, Phoebe, who loves Pollux but kills herself when she believes him dead, I'm more invested in the two brothers. Laurent's pain is so palpable, as if it's Théo he's trying to bring back to life.

When the curtain falls, there's a thunderous applause. The house may not be full, but everyone loved it. Hopefully, with the right reviews, they'll have more audience for the rest of the run.

After the opera, there's a reception in the old dancers' foyer. Ghosts and the living mix here, which means lots of practice for me. Luckily, I've got Voltaire making the rounds to meet adoring fans. I hope he remembers to ask my questions instead of just prancing around.

As for me, I desperately need to go to the toilet. As I sit in the stall, listening to the muffled buzz of chatter outside, I suddenly hear music. It's the same EDM music I heard before.

I almost jump off the toilet seat, flush, and wash my hands, hoping the music is still there. It is. As I leave the bathroom, the music leads me down a corridor. There's a door with restricted access, but I'm too curious to pay much attention to the warning.

Should I wait for Sébastien? I decide not to risk losing the music and follow it backstage. On and on it leads me until I reach the dressing rooms behind the stage. Just when I think I've found the source of the music, it stops.

In the corridor in front of me is a door with shiny red letters. I take the last two steps towards it and gasp.

The paint is still so fresh it glistens and runs down the door in blood-like streaks. A gruesome message awaits me: *The motive was jealousy.*

CHAPTER 20

I t doesn't take long to learn the door is for the dressing room of the murdered soprano. The police have shut down the opening night party—at least for the living—and are now investigating. Like the cast and crew, Sébastien and I were asked to stay. I had to tell the police how I got backstage, claiming to have taken a wrong turn, and confirm that I hadn't touched anything. They still want to take my fingerprints at the station later. A simple routine, Sébastien assures me.

Now they're questioning the cast and crew again, when they should be talking to the ghosts, as they seem much more talkative.

"I'm telling you, it's the Phantom!" says an upset violinist. "He's come back to haunt us."

A dancer's eyes widen. "I saw him watching from box five. Skull face and all."

Five? That was right next to us.

"Did you see anything?" I ask Sébastien through a half-closed mouth.

"The Phantom? No, I was too distracted by the presence of freaking Voltaire in our box."

Speaking of Voltaire, he's paying his compliments to Le Maure. A crowd has formed around the two of them. On the other side of the room, Pélissier stands surrounded by her supporters, staring daggers at her rival.

"So how did you find the message?" Sébastien asks.

"I heard the music again."

"The EDM?"

I nod. "It was coming from the walls, like before. Actually, it was coming from the dressing room."

He raises an eyebrow. "Did you go in?"

Fortunately, I didn't leave any fingerprints. "The music stopped before I got there."

"So you're saying it led you there? It wanted you to find the message?"

"That's a given. I just don't know why. Let's say it was the Phantom of the Opera. Why does he want me to see all this?" First the murder on stage, now the revelation of the motive. Not to mention Théo's "accident". "If I were the murderer, I wouldn't want anyone on my trail. Certainly not a random person with no connection to the opera. I look at Sébastien. "You know why, don't you?" I need him to confirm my theory.

Sébastien sighs heavily. "It could be a warning."

My arms are already crossed over my chest, but I still tremble. "Do you think someone would go so far as to kill a poor woman who has nothing to do with me, just to send a message? Who would do that?" I know who I'm thinking of, but I want Sébastien to say it.

Instead, he shakes his head. "It doesn't make sense. If my father wanted to kill you, he'd just do it." A frightening thought. "There's no need to involve anyone else. He certainly doesn't go around killing innocent people."

"He kill—"

Sébastien interrupts, "He turned me into a ghost whisperer."

I don't know if he said that for someone else's benefit or because he's in denial about his consensual murder. "Sure, let's go with that. I'm just saying he's certainly not above it. You know, for the safety of our country."

Sébastien snorts. "What's that got to do with a soprano?"

"Maybe she was also an undocumented ghost whisperer." That's not a bad idea, actually. My theory has its flaws, but this would solve it. "GoPol wants me to know what happens to ghost whisperers."

"Not GoPol. My father."

I keep conflating his father with the whole agency, but so far, I have very little else to go by. "Emanuelle must have thwarted his plans worse than I did." Judging by Sébastien's expression, I set the bar pretty high. "It could be!"

"Sure, but you're forgetting one thing." He gives me an apologetic smile. "My father isn't jealous of you."

"He might be." I'm not ready to give up my theory just yet.

Irritated, Sébastien steps in front of me, blocking my view of the room. "How?"

"Well, He could be jealous I have revolutionary generals on my side. That I've got the whole bloody Panthéon on my side." I shrug. "That's why you originally tried to hire me, isn't it?"

It makes him think, at least. "I wouldn't exactly call it jealousy. I mean, assuming C-Trente wrote the message—"

"Can he do that?" Just the thought of C-Trente in the same building as me sends a shiver down my spine.

"Write a message? Yes, it would take a lot of energy, but it's possible. In any case, *assuming* he did it, assuming he wanted you to find it and shake with fear… why write such a message?"

True, his father and his whisper ghost aren't above a little murder, but they'd never admit to being jealous of a history student's ghost friends. It's too petty, even for them.

"That motive doesn't really fit Madame Pirot either, does it?"

Sébastien shakes his head. "Not really, but on the other hand we'd already assumed the killer could still be around. And maybe they just want to make sure they're not misunderstood."

"Oh yes, that would be the worst thing."

He chuckles. "People are weird. Compared to the stuff I have to deal with sometimes, this is pretty tame. There are a lot of people who want to be acknowledged for their atrocities."

We've never talked about the spy work he does. I don't even know if he was working on anything other than the Chevalier before I came along. I guess that's the point, though, so I don't pester him for details.

"Anyway. Much like an academic theory, you can't base your hypothesis on who you want the perpetrator to be. An investigation is a careful collection of all the facts. Autopsies, obtaining evidence, establishing motives, interviews. You gather all the information you need to get to your suspect. That's why it takes so long."

"They didn't take long to arrest Madame Pirot."

"But they did it because of her fingerprints on the dress." He nods towards the backstage entrance. "This changes things. There's a new lead with new evidence. It might lead them to another suspect. It might not. But you can't start with the suspect and then try to fit all the pieces into your theory."

I sigh heavily. "So I suppose that's why they haven't arrested the other soprano? Alexandra Briot?"

Sébastien beams at me like a proud papa. "That's right. People have been quick to point fingers, and I'm sure she's on the list, but just because she didn't like Emanuelle or fought with her over roles doesn't mean she'd murder her."

"Even if the motive fits?" That would have nothing to do with me, but it probably makes more sense.

"Assuming what's written in red is true."

I groan as he tears that theory apart, too. Of course he's right. Who says the motive is jealousy just because it was written on the door? "This is too exhausting." Sébastien might have compared it to my academic work, but I prefer working with old texts and ghosts to living people.

Sébastien chuckles. "You wanted to do this for Garnier."

"I know—"

"Alix!" Théo's found me, ploughing through half a dozen ghosts to get to me. "They said you found it?"

I don't think I did much finding myself, but I nod for his sake. "Yes. They say it was Emanuelle's dressing room."

"You really have the worst luck when you go to the opera." Théo laughs nervously before looking sideways at Sébastien.

"Well, this is my friend from university, Théo," I tell Sébastien, although I'm sure he's already guessed as much. "And this is my boyfriend."

"Sébastien Roubert, nice to meet you." They shake hands and I see Théo wince.

"Likewise," he says, a little strained. "Are you a student, too?"

Sébastien shakes his head. "National security."

Théo's eyes widen. "Really?" When Sébastien gives him a non-committal nod, he swallows. "Well... I'm sure you'll be able to leave soon. I mean, you can probably just tell them to let you go or something. I..." He looks over his shoulder, seemingly desperate to find someone else to talk to. "I'll see if I can—"

"It was you!" a scream tears through the room, so loud I jump. "You supported that Alexandra woman, and you couldn't see her fade away like she deserves. That woman has no soul."

My heart skips a beat when I realise it's Marie Pélissier shouting at the top of her lungs. Théo's already frowning at me. "Everything okay?"

"I would never. You just wanted Mademoiselle Visse for your side to make up for your god-awful voice," Le Maure shrieks.

"My voice is perfectly fine!" There's a chorus of support for her claim, which is immediately met with just as much shouting from the other side.

"Alix?"

A fight breaks out. Ghosts go head-to-head and all sorts of things fly around. A pointe shoe is thrown straight at my face. Just before I can duck, Sébastien's arm lands on my hip, turning me into him. I gasp in pain as the pointe shoe bounces off my shoulder.

Then I'm in Sébastien's arms again and he whispers into my hair, "It's alright, Alix. I'll get you out of here." He says louder to Théo. "I think events are finally catching up with her. You're right, I should ask if we can be released." Then he whispers to me again, "Breathe, just concentrate on your breathing. It'll make the images go away."

I doubt anything can make the ghosts disappear, but Sébastien starts navigating us out of the room without giving us away. Instead of ducking, he takes another prop to the head, barely flinching, while his feet take the safest, most natural route. Fortunately, we've been standing close to the wall, so we don't have to go through where most of the ghosts are pulling hair, sinking teeth, and shoving each other around.

Once, we have to stop because two ghosts in front of us are smashing each other's heads into the wall—which doesn't have quite the impact if they both go through. Sébastien takes the opportunity to reassure me that everything's going to be fine. We pretend I'm suffering from post-traumatic shock, and it works surprisingly well. After a brief explanation from Sébastien and a show of his badge, the policeman at the door lets us out. There are definitely advantages to having a GoPol boyfriend.

When we're finally outside, breathing in the fresh air, I gasp. "Did it work?"

Sébastien puts his arm around my back. "Your friend might be a bit worried, but no one else paid us much attention. As for our imaginary friends, they were pretty busy."

"That was close."

"Extremely close." He scoffs. "What were they fighting about, anyway?"

With a sigh, I explain the whole rivalry between Pélissier and Le Maure. "It sounds to me like they're projecting their own problems onto this pair of modern-day rivals. And since this is a place of power..."

"...they may have driven them to action," Sébastien surmises. "Like Molay, who drove every overnight guest in the Boutique mad."

And how my ghosts in the Panthéon repel all those who would do me harm. But that's a secret I can't tell Sébastien. He mustn't know where I've hidden Petite Alix, for the sake of my safety and his integrity. So I just say, "Exactly. I know I'm doing it the wrong way, but Alexandra had the motive and the access, and with Le Maure taking her jealousy up a few notches, she might have done something she never would've considered otherwise. Like kill an up-and-coming rival before she could sideline her."

"I've never heard of anything like that, but then I haven't heard of a lot of things that have happened lately." He looks at me and brushes a stray hair from my cheek. "You have this effect of making me question everything I've learnt."

I know he won't be able to admit what he learnt was wrong, let alone that he was deliberately led astray so he too would see ghosts as nothing more than tools. Perhaps the key to his heart doesn't lie in forcing a rebellion, because that's far too frightening. What Sébastien needs isn't insecurity and threats, but hope. Hope that the things he believes in, like national security, can be achieved in a different way. A much less traumatic way.

"What if it worked? What if my way worked as well as yours? Maybe even better?"

He swallows hard. "How?"

"Remember our first meeting? Our second meeting, actually, in the restaurant, before Cédric and Hélène invited themselves to our table." I take a moment to collect my thoughts as he nods. "You told me every ghost whisperer has a few close relationships, but that many of your ghosts get bored and can't be trusted. Which is why you rely so heavily on your whisper ghosts."

"What are you getting at?"

"Well, how close are these relationships really? Leaving aside the police officers and their sense of duty, what motivates the ghosts to work for you? Like you said, they get bored easily."

Understanding dawns on him. "But if we build real relationships, see them as friends, and help them as much as we want them to help us, they could become much more reliable. Because then they'd care. But we have to care first." Someone's been listening to Voltaire.

A smile spreads across my lips as he understands. "Look, I'm not saying the power of friendship solves everything. But wouldn't it be worth a try? Even if it doesn't significantly improve your success rate, what's the worst that could happen? You make a few friends? Make the world if not a safer place, then at least a kinder one?"

Sébastien chuckles softly. "You really are something else."

"You could be, too."

He swallows and averts his eyes. "I'm not so sure of that."

Instinctively, I take his hand and force his eyes back to my face. "Well, I *am*. You could, Sébastien. I truly believe you could."

CHAPTER 21

The next day Gaby, Marie, and I visit Gaspar's grave. I've got Malou in my bag, hoping her ghost-sniffing skills will work where mine might not. At the moment she's asleep, making the sweetest kind of snore. As we ride the Métro towards the cemetery, I fill Gaby and Marie in on what happened at the opera, omitting any mention of ghosts in case anyone is listening.

"Oh, that reminds me, I haven't told you about Théo yet." How is it that Sébastien knows the whole story and my best friend doesn't? I quickly fill Gaby in and feel vindicated when she gasps in outrage.

"What is he? Five? I thought the whole teasing the girl you like thing was done and dusted in primary school? What an idiot."

"I know! It was so awkward. Besides, I don't think he really likes me, just..." I can't find the right words to express my feelings.

Fortunately, Gaby comes through for me. "A version of you. The clean, uncomplicated version. What he wants is a pretty girl with a good head on her shoulders and both feet firmly planted in this world. You're so much more than that. You need a real man who can appreciate you. Like Gaspar."

"Like Sébastien," Marie says at the same time and giggles. "Maybe you need two men to appreciate all of you."

I roll my eyes and scoff at her. "That sounds like I'm just too much to handle."

Gaby takes my hands and stares at me. "If a man can't handle all sides of you, then he's not worth the ground beneath your feet." She clicks her tongue. "See, that's why I can't be bothered with men."

Marie laughs again, then leans into Gaby's side. "They have their advantages. Not many, but some."

"If you say so."

"Oh, we have to get out!" Somehow we've lost track of time and have just arrived at the Edgar Quinet Métro station.

We jump from our seats and run for the exit, barely making it before the door closes behind us. Once we've recovered from the shock, the three of us burst into laughter.

"That was close," Gaby says, wiping tears from the corners of her eyes. "Alright." She turns to find the right exit. "Let's go see your boyfriend."

I love the way she says it, as if there's no way he's not at his grave. "Okay."

We leave the Métro station on Boulevard Edgar Quinet and quickly find the main entrance to Montparnasse. It's the second largest cemetery in Paris, with around 35,000 graves. A long time ago this was all farmland. Today, the only remnant is the Moulin de la Charité, an old mill tower in the middle of the cemetery. For a long time, it was the caretaker's house, but now it's empty and can be visited by tourists.

Like all the other cemeteries, it's a spacious area with trees of all kinds. It doesn't have the wide avenues of Père Lachaise or the beautiful backdrop of Montmartre, but it's still a hotspot for grave tourists. One of the most visited graves is that of Jean-Paul Sartre and Simone de Beauvoir, both 20th century existentialist philosophers who lived in a scandalously open relationship. Back then, the scandal was more about their rejection of marriage and their numerous affairs with other people. Today, the scandal is rooted in the MeToo movement, as many of their so-called affairs were actually underage and groomed. It's a complicated issue in a culture that considers "seduction" one of its finest arts.

"Don't tell me you're friends with them," Gaby says in disgust.

"I don't go to Montparnasse very often, and no, I've never spoken to them." That's the trouble with ghosts sometimes. They all come with values and ideas that we've shed, or should shed, as soon as possible. I find it hard to blame most of them for the kind of society they grew up in. Some have managed to move on, but many are still stuck in their old ways. Then again, their old ways were often centuries ago, so it feels a bit petty to judge them after all this time. Some things like this, though... I just don't want to get involved in, big contributions to society or not.

Marie takes the lead, navigating past the many rows of graves. I try to ignore everyone else, not even bothering to distinguish between ghosts and the living, by concentrating on Gaby. Finally, we stop in front of an incredibly fancy mausoleum with an old, weathered inscription. *On ne meurt jamais vraiment, tant qu'on ne nous oublie pas*: we never really die, as long as we're not forgotten.

I shudder as the truth of the epitaph sinks in. Is it just the vain hope of leaving a lasting legacy, or did whoever built it know something about the mechanics of the afterlife?

It's a beautiful mausoleum: white marble with two caring angel statues guarding the interior, and a decorative wrought-iron gate. And it's big. One of the biggest in this row, with more family tombs in front of it. It takes me a whole minute before I realise we didn't stop here by chance.

"This is Gaspar's family?" Not all the ghosts are there, but the few that are drifting through the garden glare at me.

Marie nods. "Fancy, isn't it? I mean, I knew he came from a wealthy family, but I found it all a bit overwhelming. Gustave and I felt quite out of place. He had one of those really elaborate funerals. Awfully long. Didn't feel like him at all."

I remember Gaspar telling me about his family. How they cared more about their reputation than anything else. He must've hated such a formal funeral. And I wasn't even there to help him through it. Worst girlfriend ever.

Marie points to a grave in the second row on the left. "That's his. I guess the crypt is full or something."

Or only reserved for those who haven't dragged the family name, *du Charbonneau*, through the mud.

Ignoring the haughty ghosts around me, I make my way to Gaspar's grave.

GASPAR EMILIEN DU CHARBONNEAU

5.3.2002–14.10.2023

Fils bien-aimé de François & Josette

That's it. As far as I know, he grew up in a cold and distant home. And that his father was ashamed of his son studying sociology. Beloved son, my ass.

A hand falls on my shoulder. Startled, I blink away tears and look into Gaby's eyes. "Is he here?"

"No." The grave is as empty as the words on it. I decide not to read too much into it and crouch down to grab Malou. "You know what would've made a better epigraph?" I say to the little sleepyhead. "'Beloved hedgehog boy and music enthusiast'. 'He wanted to make the world a better place'." I snort. "Or maybe 'Only the good die young'." Okay, that last one's a bit of a cliché, but it's true. I bet none of the ghosts around me cared one bit about the underprivileged.

I set Malou on the cold ground and she snuffs angrily. "Pardon, ma puce. I'll put you back where it's warm soon. Just try to pick up a sniff of Gaspar. You know him, don't you? He gave you a great cuddle."

"Not as good as mine," jokes Gaby, while Marie coos, "She's so sweet."

But Malou doesn't pick up anything, either. She's not interested in the grave and keeps coming back to me, trying to climb back into my bag. With a sigh, I cross off that avenue and put her back in her warm place, wrapping a scarf around her for good measure.

Not quite sure what else to do, I call out to him again. "Gaspar, please come back. I need you."

The ghosts around me mutter. They want me gone and find it absurd I should know one of their own. Others claim they always knew he was doomed and ran with the wrong crowd. As if only delinquents get knocked off their bikes on the morning commute. It pains me that Gaspar's final resting place is among such a condescending crowd. I bet this is the last place he'd want to spend any part of his afterlife. But if not here, where else can I look for him?

After a while, someone tugs on my sleeve. "Do we have to leave?" I glare to the side, but instead of Gaby I see a girl in a long white dress. Two brown braids fall over her shoulders. She looks innocent, on the brink of womanhood, but still a child. Judging by her nightdress, she died at least a hundred and fifty years ago. "What is it?"

She glances at the older ghosts, as if afraid of getting reprimanded. "He's gone."

I swallow hard as she repeats what I know so well. "You knew Gaspar?"

"He's a descendant of my younger brother Simón. The main line of the family. It died with Gaspar."

Gaby crouches next to me, half sitting in the girl, who moves aside. She smiles and says, "Of course I did."

Being the great friend she is, she's covering for me. Gratefully, I face the girl. "That's sad." Although I have very unfriendly feelings towards Gaspar's family, I recognise the loss of tradition. Another old family gone. It's a silly thought, really, they weren't anything special, but not many have a family mausoleum. Now only two more plots will be filled, maybe more if he still has living grandparents. And then no one but tourists will give the noble Charbonneau family more than a passing glance. I look up at the inscription on the mausoleum and sigh. If that happens, they'll really be dead one day, forgotten by everyone.

"No, you don't understand." The girl shakes her head, then looks back over her shoulder. She bites her lip nervously. "He's not here anymore." She lowers her voice. "They dug him up."

CHAPTER 22

Shocked, I stare at the girl with the big brown eyes that look a little like Gaspar's. Slowly, I make sense of her words. "They dug him up?" A nod. "Who did?"

She shrugs. "Two men dressed in black. They came at night. They were very quick, like they'd done it a hundred times. He hasn't been back since."

I'm starting to tremble. There's only one reason I can think of why someone would dig up his body. To scatter his bones. To tear him apart, like we had to do with Molay, like those unfortunate souls in the catacombs. My heart's squeezed dry as the image of the disjointed ghosts comes back to me. They'd all lost their identities, remembered enough to stay in this world, but not enough to be themselves. If they've scattered Gaspar's bones, he's even less than that.

Gaby puts an arm around me. "Hey, darling. Maybe it's best if we go."

"I agree," says a harsh-looking ghost nearby. "You've long overstayed your welcome, whisperer."

A sudden shiver runs down my spine and I stumble to my feet, needing Gaby to steady me. I shouldn't have spoken to the girl. Shouldn't have even acknowledged her. What if these ghosts are on GoPol's payroll? I can only hope that after collecting Gaspar's bones, GoPol will have no reason to come back and check in with them. On the other hand, what if I've just walked into a trap? I didn't react to Garnier when he was in my face or to C-Trente when he was drilling into me, but I fell for the innocent-looking girl.

I stagger away from the crypt and down the path, feeling as if GoPol officers are about to descend on me. Trap or punishment. Which one is it?

"Alix?" Gaby has wrapped her arm around mine. "What happened?"

"They took him. GoPol took him." Tears run down my cheeks as I acknowledge the harsh truth. "He's gone, Gaby. He's really gone."

She pulls me into a hug without a moment's hesitation. I wrap my arms around her back and cry into her shoulder. "It's all my fault. If he hadn't got involved with me... If I hadn't upset them..." Gaspar was my willing accomplice, but I still feel like I brought him down. He was already dead, and now he can't even enjoy his afterlife. No, they had to destroy him. Just to punish me.

"Oh, sweetheart." Gaby strokes my back. "I don't know what to say."

All this time I've clung to hope. Clung to it like a vine to a crumbling mansion. Now it's lying shattered on the muddy ground in all its useless glory. Gaspar is gone. I've really lost him this time.

Even though it's only two in the afternoon, I feel exhausted. I want to crawl into bed and stay there for the rest of the month. Unfortunately, I don't get that kind of mercy. Ten minutes from home I get a message from Maman: *When are you back?*

I reply: *Soon*, and receive an embarrassing smiley face.

Ten minutes later, I walk through the door and am immediately called into the living room. My parents and Odile are sitting around the table, sharing Maman's macarons and a pot of coffee. I still want to cry in my room, but perhaps it'd be better to spend some time with my family. They're such a contrast to Gaspar's cold relatives I suddenly feel the need to appreciate them more.

"Where have you been?" Maman asks with a warm smile.

"Just hanging out with Gaby." I've long since learnt that cemeteries don't make the best conversation pieces.

I hang my bag on the chair and take Malou out. Odile snatches her up immediately and coos at her sleepy form. "Did you have a nice walk, ma puce?" Odile coos.

"She didn't like it very much."

Odile gives me a sharp look. "It's cold and in the middle of the day. Of course she didn't like it." She makes a nest in her hoodie and puts Malou inside. "I'll keep you warm."

My mother's still smiling at me. "So, no fancy boyfriend date today?" There's a twinkle in her eye, which tells me she's already too invested.

"He's certainly making an effort to be fancy," says Papa, not quite as impressed. "Do you even like the opera? I don't know if I would've gone back so soon after what happened two weeks ago."

"That was the point, you know? To take the sting out of it before it turns into something it doesn't need to be. People don't get murdered on stage every day, Papa."

He's about to answer when the doorbell rings and excuses himself.

Maman pushes her macarons towards me. "Have one, dear."

I don't need to be asked twice. Her macarons are the best. Just as I've got my mouth full of chewy pastry and creamy goodness, my father returns with Hélène in tow. I almost choke on my macaron. Instead, I cough and spit a few flakes on my lips. Embarrassed, I cover my mouth and quickly swallow the rest. When I'm somewhat presentable, I ask, "What's this?"

My sister gives me an equally cold look. Unlike me, she doesn't question it and greets first our mother and then Odile with kisses. I'm overlooked, which suits me just fine. Unfortunately, the only chair available at the table is next to mine. Surely an oversight by design.

Hélène falters ever so slightly. Still ignoring me, she sits down and picks up a macaron. "Oh, these look amazing, Maman."

"Coffee?" Maman asks, pot in hand. When Hélène nods at her, she asks me, "You too, Alix?"

Am I the only one who feels weird about this? It's not the first time we've had afternoon tea as a family. It was a regular event when Hélène lived here, and even more so when she came to visit. And yet I feel trapped. One look at Odile tells me she knows exactly what's going on, but when she catches my eye, she suddenly becomes very interested in Malou, and I begin to think that's been her plan all along.

Maman takes my lack of reaction as approval and a moment later I'm trapped by sweets and coffee next to Hélène. "I've missed this," she says with a smile that's just a little too wide. "We haven't done this for so long, have we, mon chér?"

Papa puts his hand on hers. The front is united. "Indeed. It's nice to have all our girls together in one place."

"I've missed this, too," Hélène replies like the eager sycophant she is. "I've been so buried in wedding preparations, it's nice to take a breather."

Odile and I remain silent, not in the mood to add to the pretence.

"Is there anything I can do to help?" Maman asks.

"There are still a few people who haven't RSVP'd yet. I need to finalise the numbers by the end of next week, so if you'd like to carefully follow up with some relatives, I wouldn't mind," Hélène suggests. "Otherwise, it's all going according to plan. I've got the dress"—bought without me—"the food and accommodation are arranged, the flowers are booked. I still have to get some decorations, but I'll do that next week with a friend."

I wonder if this friend is the new witness. If so, it didn't take long for Hélène to replace me. Or perhaps my official demotion was long overdue.

Unfortunately, that's what we're going to talk about. "We want you to have a wonderful wedding, Léni, so if you need anything, just let us know," Maman says with a hand on Hélène's. Then she looks at me. "It's a big moment for the whole family, so... I know you have a lot of feelings about this, Alix, but with the wedding only a month away, don't you think it's time you two made up?"

This isn't afternoon tea. It's a bloody intervention.

"You're right, Maman," Hélène says sweetly. "I want this day to be perfect. Cédric is the love of my life. He's a wonderful partner. Unfortunately, Alix can't see that. She hates him more than anything. Why should I invite someone who wants us to split up?"

The whole time, she never looks at me. It's as if I don't exist.

Instead of protesting, I put down my macaron and say, "It's alright, really. I don't want to be there." My throat tightens a little as I add, "Or here."

When I try to stand up, my father gives me a stern look. "Alix, please. We're all adults. We can talk this out."

This is so unfair. "We talked. Hélène won't listen. She's too stubborn to even consider I might not be completely deranged."

"I never said you were deranged."

It's the first time she's looked at me and I scoff. "You said I needed help. Mental help."

"And I still think you do, but not my circus, not my monkeys. I refuse to let you ruin my happiness." And just like that, Hélène turns her head away from me and smiles sweetly at our parents.

Maman sighs and massages her eyebrows before continuing. "I see there's a lot to unpack here. Let's make it a rule not to throw accusations at each other, okay?" Her eyes land on me. "Why don't you like Cédric, darling? He's such a nice man, always so considerate. I thought the two of you were friends."

"Why would you think that?" There's no universe in which we ever were or ever will be friends.

"Well, he's always cared for you."

"That's true," Hélène chimes in. "He tried very hard to get along with Alix and Odi. Family is so important to him."

I feel like throwing up. "He didn't *care* about me. He took a special interest in me."

"Oh, please! You're reading too much into it," Hélène protests.

"He sold me out. He worked on me until I trusted him just enough, and then he sold me out to secure his new fancy promotion. That was the only interest he ever had in me, and you played right into his hands."

"Sold you out?" Maman asks, her brow furrowed. "Alix, don't you think you're being a bit overdramatic? I'm sure he got this promotion on his own merits. I mean, since when have you had anything to do with the police?"

Hélène turns to me triumphantly, crossing her arms. "Yes, Alix, since when?"

"Alix," my mother says more sternly, picking up on Hélène's provocative tone, "is there something you want to tell us?"

Just then, Papa puts a hand on hers. "Careful, Marguerite. Remember, we're not taking sides." He flicks me a nervous glance, and I get the feeling that he might possibly be a little bit on my side.

But my mother has always been on Hélène's side. They're two peas in a pod, so sensible and overly concerned with my activities.

"I had to bail Alix out of jail," Hélène blurts out.

I stare at her in shock. Somehow this feels even worse than when she threw me out of her car in the pouring rain. Sisters don't rat each other out. They fight, kick, and scratch, but when it comes to their parents, they keep their mouths shut.

"Alix," Maman snaps, forgetting all about not taking sides. "Is that true?"

"There are no charges. I was just in the wrong place at the wrong time."

"You mean in the catacombs," Hélène doubles down. "You're lucky they didn't charge you with trespassing. Cédric said there was more, but he put in a good word and his boss decided to deal with it privately."

His boss certainly did that. Or so he thought, when he ordered Sébastien to destroy my whisper ghost.

Under the table, out of everyone's sight, I feel Odile's hand on my knee. She's the only one who knows what really happened, but I don't blame her for staying out of it. I'd do the same if I could.

As Papa watches my face with growing concern, nervously licking his lips, Maman gasps for air. "What's going on, Alix? Please."

Tears sting my eyes, but I refuse to cry. Hélène doesn't deserve it. "You want to know what's going on? For real?"

Hélène rolls her eyes and moans. "Don't listen to her, Maman. They're the most blatant lies."

She's gone too far this time. My mother gives her a withering look and declares, "I will *listen*." When she looks at me, a muscle in her cheek twitches, but her eyes are kind.

Any smugness I might've felt is crushed under the heavy weight that settles on my shoulders. Maman doesn't believe in ghosts. It's only been a few months since she tried to get me into therapy. I don't know if I'm strong enough to open myself up to her scrutiny and disbelief. But then I catch my father's eye. He nods, letting me know he'll support me with the truth.

Still, I must be careful and keep my emotions in check. I can't let Hélène know that I haven't suffered the consequences she thinks I have.

Odile's grip on my knee tightens as I speak. "I wasn't involved with the police. I was picked up by GoPol, the ghost police."

Although she'd seen the GoPol name on the building at the New Year's Eve party, my mother didn't know what it stood for. "Ghost police?" she repeats, unable to keep the worry from her face. I see her gripping my father's fingers tightly. She must be thinking I genuinely need help.

"I know you believe it's all in my head, but Odile and even Hélène can confirm ghosts are real."

Obviously, Hélène is not going to do that. She folds her arms over her chest and stares stubbornly ahead. Odile's muffled confirmation does little to help my case.

Instead, it's Papa who speaks up for me. "It's true, Marguerite. I saw them too—for a brief moment. The ghosts are the souls of everyone who died. They look like us and I..." His voice falters. "I wasn't well when I saw them. Alix is much stronger than I was. Luckily, Cédric took me to the GoPol headquarters and they—"

"Took your ghost away."

Papa winces as if I've slapped him. "I asked for it."

I can see how confused Maman is. Irritated, she looks at my father. "What are you talking about, Rémy?"

"Ghosts are all around us," I explain. "They live on, invisible to most of us. I can see them because my heart stopped when I was three." As expected, Maman gasps. She'd tried so hard to keep it from me. "That created what's called a whisper ghost, which used to keep me tethered to the other side." There, I got the tense right.

"Yeah, but the problem is that Alix treats ghosts like real people," Hélène chimes in. "She's completely lost sight of the line between life and death, putting her own life at risk for all these dead people. She even had a dead boyfriend."

Having just visited Gaspar's grave and finding it desecrated, that one hits particularly hard. I hate that it's happening, but the tears finally roll down my cheeks.

"What's wrong with a ghost boyfriend?" Odile asks, opening her mouth properly for the first time.

"Sébastien's dead?" Maman asks.

"No, Maman," Hélène assures her. "He's alive. She had another one before. Gaston or something."

"Gaspar!" She can't even remember his name. "And thanks to your *wonderful* fiancé, he's been taken away from me. So, thanks for that!"

Hélène doesn't seem to care. She just shrugs her shoulders and turns up her nose, as if Gaspar was never a real person.

I glare at Maman. "No, I'm *not* being overdramatic. The ghosts were my friends. I have real relationships with them, and they've helped me in many ways. Some have even saved my life. But the ghost police didn't like that, so they came after me. And Cédric betrayed me because all he ever wanted was to be a ghost whisperer like me, and he doesn't care who he has to hurt to get there. Which, to be honest, makes him a perfect fit for GoPol. Because if anyone's completely deranged, it's them."

"You're just jealous that he's actually qualified for the job," Hélène claims.

"Don't you get it? He has to *die* for the job! He won't be a ghost whisperer until his heart has stopped at least once." As soon as I mention it, the colour drains from Hélène's face. It's as if she had never stopped long enough to connect the dots.

"Alix..." my father warns, looking very uncomfortable now.

But I'm not finished. "About him helping you with your problem. I know you said it was your decision, but frankly, it wasn't a very informed decision. Cédric did a lot of gaslighting to convince you, just as he's completely gaslit Hélène." I push my chair back and put my hands on the table. "They've taken away everything I've ever cared about, so excuse me if, *no,* I don't want to play the happy family and attend Hélène's wedding to that creep. And if she continues to support him over me, then she's no longer my sister."

"Alix!" Maman calls after me, but I'm already on my way out.

I run into my room and slam the door behind me. Then I throw myself on my bed and cry bitter tears into my pillow. Fresh grief for Gaspar washes over me and I feel like I'm drowning. I've just told Hélène she's no longer my sister. No doubt she'll be all sensible and mature and win over my parents. Odile will probably take my side, but I doubt she'll last much longer at the table than I did.

Suddenly I can't breathe. I have to get out. Away from Hélène and my parents. But if I leave, I don't think I'll ever come back. My mind races, dancing around half-formed ideas. I can't move in with Gaby. She'll take me in, no question, but her flat is far too small for two people. And I don't want to get in her way with Marie all the time.

Sébastien's apartment comes to mind, but we're not at that stage in our relationship, real or fake. I doubt he wants me to turn up with suitcase in hand and take over his workout room or anything like that. The truth is, I don't have anywhere to go. Leaving now is simply not possible. It takes a calm mind, and I'm anything but.

I throw myself back onto my pillow and cry until there are no more tears left to shed. When the door finally closes behind Hélène—apparently she and my parents talked for ages after I stormed off—all I have left in me are pitiful hiccups. How could I ever hope to make my parents understand? I'm too emotional. Hysterical, some of my old-fashioned ghost friends would say. And this isn't a world for overt emotions. No, we're all forced to bottle it up and are judged when our bottles explode. Rationality is the only way to get ahead in this world. To survive.

A few minutes later, the door to my room opens. A weight settles on my bed next to my hip and a hand falls on my head, gently stroking my hair. "Oh, sweetheart." It's Maman.

Unable to acknowledge her, I press my face into the pillow, wishing it would just suffocate me so I'd no longer have to deal with the living.

"Look," Maman says quietly. "I don't claim to understand half of what's going on, but stay safe, okay?" She plants a kiss on my head. "We need you in this world."

CHAPTER 23

The next day I still feel incredibly raw, but a chat with Gaby and Odile's declaration over breakfast that she's firmly on my side have helped to take the sting out of it. For the moment, Hélène is dead to me. Not literally, because then she'd be a ghost and see the world more clearly. But figuratively, I'm done with her. Let her marry Cédric. They were made for each other.

Luckily, today's a work day for me. As soon as I set foot in the Panthéon, I feel like coming home. Here's my ghost family who are firmly on my side. And unlike my real family, there won't be any surprise interventions questioning the very core of my being. Maybe I should move here.

Who am I kidding? I'll never move here. Not while I'm alive, and certainly not when I'm dead.

Voltaire is waiting for me in the staff room, looking like he's got important news.

"Talk to me during the tour, okay?"

Unlike Jean-Jacques Rousseau, who often talks my ear off while I'm trying to give my tour of the Panthéon, Voltaire does it more cleverly, using the many breaks in the tour when my guests are exploring the various areas on their own. "From what I've heard, the conflict between the Pélissiens and the Mauriens has only grown since their deaths. Many of their followers have joined one side or the other only after their deaths. There's hardly a ghost in the whole opera who doesn't side with one of the two sopranos. That's how strong their rivalry is. In a way, it is the heart of the opera. The magic of the place."

My memories of the ghostly brawl don't exactly exude magic, but I understand what Voltaire means. The two divas represent what opera used to be all about: larger-than-life singers, inflated egos, and more glamour than substance. It was a place of luxury, a pastime for the upper classes. Who can name a contemporary opera singer? I'd never heard of Alexandra Briot or Emanuelle Visse before reading the evening's programme. Don't get me wrong. They are still incredible singers, but they don't have the same flair as a Marie Pélissier or Catherine-Nicole le Maure.

I give my talk on Foucalt's Pendulum, while Voltaire waits patiently. As soon as the group disperses around the giant pendulum, he continues, "With each ghost who's joined the opera, the conflict has grown. So, we're looking at almost three hundred years of petty fighting. Now, twice in the history of the Paris Opera, things have taken a turn for the worse."

"Twice?" I immediately cover my mouth and cough as the word slips from my lips.

"Yes, once in the late 19th century, shortly after the opening of the Palais Garnier. You know the story." Since I can't speak, Voltaire confirms it himself. "The Phantom of the Opera. The names were different, but they're a little blurred now. The problem with what the living remember, as you know. Pélissier supported Carlotta and Le Maure took Christine under her wing."

I suppose what he's trying to say is that there was a similar conflict, which Gaston Leraux borrowed heavily from, but the names of those sopranos are no longer remembered, and instead their fictional identities have been imprinted on them. Ghosts can be so confusing sometimes.

"Well, while the Phantom was a living person, Pélissier told me he could see ghosts. Most of the things he pulled off were pure engineering genius and parlour tricks, but he also had help from his whisper ghost. Most importantly, he was able to take the conflict between the two sopranos and spin it into a deadly web. As you know, it has cost the lives of several people."

So far, only one person has died. Is there another phantom in the opera? I think of Garnier's "unnatural presence". Unnatural as in people who bridge the worlds of the living and the dead? People like me?

I take my group down to the crypt and give them brief introductions to the various ghosts down there. I'm usually more playful about this, but I'm eager to hear more about what Voltaire has to say.

"The ghostly activity died down when the Phantom, Christine, and her whining lover boy turned their backs on the opera. The conflict lived on, but the lack of a real rivalry to mirror the ghosts diminished everyone's influence. They simply need the drama to thrive. Things heated up when Emanuelle Visse joined the company. At first, no one thought much of her, but soon her star began to rise and before long she was considered a contender for the leading role that Alexandra Briot had dominated for years.

"As I'm sure you've heard, when these unbearable women started to blame each other, this time Le Maure preferred the old soprano, while Pélissier took a liking to the young Mademoiselle Visse. After a few years, all this negative energy began to seep back into the living world." He shakes his head. "I've said it before and I'll say it again, both women are exceptional artists. I don't understand this need to declare one superior to the other."

Coming from the man who had his own memorable feud and now exists in close proximity to his rival, it's a bit rich. I can't count how many times Voltaire and Rousseau have had their differences. But for me, they've come together.

A thought manifests itself in my mind. The opera ghosts were once negatively influenced by a ghost whisperer. I don't want to put too much stock in myself, but I'd say compared to a lunatic murderer in the walls, I'm a pretty positive influence. Perhaps all the opera ghosts need is the kind of person who can bring them together and heal the rift that's been growing for three hundred years.

Yeah, I'm not up for that job. Maybe in the distant future, when GoPol is no longer breathing down my neck. Besides, according to Voltaire, there might already be a ghost whisperer in the opera. Someone who has more in common with the Phantom than me.

"Excuse me?" asks a tourist. I've completely forgotten about my group. "Could you tell us more about Marie Curie? I've always admired her."

So have I. From afar.

With a sigh, I put on my guide smile and welcome them to approach Pierre and Marie's tomb. "Of course. She lived a life as amazing as it was tragic. Did you know her husband died in a freak accident only ten years after they were married?"

Voltaire doesn't have much to add. As far as Pélissier knows, there's no whisper ghost. She *did* confirm the "unnatural presence", but according to her, this presence has only recently taken up residence, while the accidents and mishaps have been going on for years.

Two, to be exact.

I finish my shift and close the Panthéon. It's been a good day's work, even if my thoughts have been all over the place and I've probably given the worst tours in a long time. But the tourists and ghosts kept me busy. Now that it's time to go home, the uneasy feeling is back. Maybe I'll ask Gaby if she's up for a sleepover. But only if she's not already on a date with Marie.

Phone in hand, I lock the side door and start down the stairs. I feel it before I see it.

A cold, oil-like fear runs down my spine and it takes all my willpower not to meet his eyes. Philippe's story comes back to me. A man asking for me. I should have known it'd be him.

A sick smile on his lips, C-Trente crosses the square, heading for the stairs I've half descended.

I allow myself a tiny breath before gasping for air. "Oh crap." Then I spin on my heels and run up the stairs. Not as fast as I would have liked, but hopefully like someone who's forgotten something and is returning quickly to get it.

"You can't run away from me," C-Trente growls.

My keys almost fall to the floor and my hands shake as I fumble through them to find the right one. Why is this so hard all of a sudden?

"She's here, right?" C-Trente says. "Your little girl. My boy's gone rogue for you, hasn't he?"

His feet hit the stairs and I still haven't managed to open the door. It's as if my muscles have decided to stop working. All that goes through my head is: *He knows, he's going to take Petite Alix away from me, he's going to...* Finally, the door opens and I hurry inside.

In a panic, I close the door and lock it behind me. Then I run to the crypt. There's no more pretending for me.

"He's here!" I gasp. "Charles Roubert's whisper ghost is here. He knows everything. He'll take her and—"

Suddenly Victor is there, his hands falling heavily on my shoulders. "Breathe, Alix."

"No, no, we need to make a plan. We have to escape. There has to be another way out. Anything."

"You'll be safe here," Victor says slowly. "Do you really think some lousy 21st century whisper ghost can get through all of us?"

The words sink in slowly, and I take a few choppy breaths. "He's outside."

Victor nods. "I can feel him. But I promise you, he won't be able to get in. And he won't be able to take Petite Alix from us." Somewhere in the crypt I hear the little one crying. I must have scared her pretty bad. "He's not nearly as strong."

"But he'll be waiting for me." I swallow hard and wipe away a few tears. "What am I going to do?" Maybe I really should move to the Panthéon. I'm sure that'd go down extremely well with my boss.

"Right now? Breathe."

As annoying as the advice is, I know he's right. A few minutes have passed and there's still no sign of C-Trente. But he *will* be waiting. If I know anything, he'll stay there all night, waiting for the moment when I'm no longer protected by my ghosts. As safe as the Panthéon is, it has now become a trap for me.

Victor gently leads me to a bench and sits down with me until I've got my breathing under control and stopped whimpering. When my head's finally cleared a little, he begins to speak. "You know we'll have you here as long as you need."

I nod. Sleeping in the Panthéon won't be any fun. There are no blankets. My uniform is barely good enough for a pillow and almost everything else is cold, unforgiving stone. And how long will C-Trente wait? He's a whisper ghost. He doesn't need to sleep, eat, or even pee. If this is his mission, and I'm sure it is, he'll be out there for as long as it takes.

"It won't work. I can't stay here for the rest of my life." That would also confirm what C-Trente already knows in his heart. As a ghost, he probably feels my pull, but he doesn't have his proof yet.

"What you need is a bodyguard," Victor muses. "Someone who can get you out of here."

There's really only one person I can think of, unless one of my ghosts offers to stay with me. And although I trust them, that would again prove C-Trente's theory. "I'll see what Sébastien can

194

do. But he might be busy." *Or unwilling to openly oppose GoPol,* I think.

My fingers are still shaking when I text him my dilemma. I expect to have to wait a while, but his reply is as quick as it is affirmative: *That damn whisper ghost. Stay there. I'm coming to get you. Don't go outside until I text you.*

Victor reads the message over my shoulder. "You're a team now?"

"Friends," I say, because at this point there's no doubt about it. We may have started this collaboration on shaky ground, but Sébastien's proven himself time and time again. He really meant it when he threw his hat in my ring.

"That's good. You need someone in your corner. Someone who lives and experiences the world the way you do."

In my opinion, Sébastien is still a long way from experiencing the world as I do, but I understand what Victor means. All my life I've been looking for others like me. Someone who understands this confusing double existence. Sébastien could be the one to satisfy this need. *If* I can get him away from his psychotic father.

It takes about twenty minutes before another text arrives: *The coast is clear.*

"That was quick." He must have been nearby or raced here.

I get up slowly and walk upstairs, half the ghosts of the Panthéon behind me. Although Victor assures me he can no longer sense

C-Trente's presence, it takes a full minute to work up the courage to unlock the door, and even then I peer carefully through the slit.

Sébastien is standing on the stairs, keeping an eye on the surroundings. As far as I can see, there's no sign of his father's ghost.

As I open the door wider, he turns and looks at me worriedly. "Sorry about that."

"Thanks for coming," I say in a meek little voice. Then I take a deep breath. "Is he gone?"

Sébastien nods. "I told him I was picking you up from work. Gave him quite a dressing-down. I'll lodge a complaint."

To whom, I want to ask, as I'm pretty sure his father has sanctioned this course of action, but I'm willing to keep his illusion intact. "Thanks."

His eyes widen as I step out. I look behind me and see Victor, Voltaire, and three generals of Napoleon's guard have followed me outside.

Victor nods at Sébastien with a stern expression that frightens even me. "I trust you will take good care of my girl."

Sébastien swallows. "Of course, Monsieur. I'll make sure nothing happens to her."

Satisfied, Victor hugs me and kisses my hair. "Remember, you can always come here."

"Thank you."

The ghosts watch us as we cross the square to where Sébastien has illegally parked his motorbike. "That was Victor Hugo, wasn't it?" Sébastien whispers in awe. "You're his girl?"

"He's one of my best friends."

"So you're not... I mean, he had a *lot* of affairs."

I grimace. "Ugh, no. He's like a father to me. His own daughter drowned in the Seine, just like me." Only I was saved in time.

Sébastien's face relaxes, and he sighs with relief. "That makes a lot more sense." He hands me the spare helmet. "Shall I take you home or..." He lets the rest peter out, too shy to suggest another option.

C-Trente could be waiting for me at home. Or Hélène. I'm not sure which is worse at the moment. "I think it'd be safer if I stayed with you."

His breath catches a little, eyes locked with mine. It takes him a moment to speak. "Agreed." Quickly, he looks away and gets on his bike. "Let's go then."

Just as I get on behind him, I receive another text message. It's from Théo: *My brother was arrested.*

CHAPTER 24

I nstead of going home, we head straight for the opera. I feel a little uneasy after C-Trente's scare, expecting him to appear behind me at any moment, but I tell myself it'll be fine. Even if he does show up, I'm just visiting a friend in need.

As far as I can tell, the matinée ended about half an hour ago. People are still standing outside, waiting for their ride. There's a certain buzz, but not what I'd expect from a crowd who's just seen the lead actor arrested. I suppose the police handled it discreetly after the curtain fell.

Théo lets us in through a side entrance and leads us into the archives. Here we're away from any onlookers or worried staff. It's a medium-sized room with lots of cupboards and filing cabinets. On the left, there's a workstation, the table littered with letters and scores. Théo closes the door behind us and immediately starts pacing.

"They took him right after curtain call. I couldn't even talk to him."

"Do you know why they arrested him?" Sébastien asks with professional interest.

"They found paint in his dressing room. The same paint that was used on the wall," says Théo, looking more desperate by the minute.

I remember how convinced Laurent was Alexandra had killed Emanuelle. The police hadn't arrested her, so it made sense for him to take matters into his own hands and try to put them on her trail. Only it backfired badly.

"So, he wrote the note," Sébastien surmises. "That's vandalism at best, not murder."

Théo stops, his breathing quick and sharp. "But that's the problem." He takes a deep breath to keep his voice from cracking. "The officer I spoke to said the killer used a blistering agent. I forget which one, but apparently it was found in the paint. The paint is the poison."

Sébastien inhales sharply. "That changes things."

"He didn't do it!" Théo whines, his face contorting in agony. "Laurent *loved* Emanuelle! He worshipped the ground she walked on."

"And Emanuelle?" Sébastien asks calmly. "How did she feel about Laurent?"

Théo swallows. "They slept together after the opening night of Medée. They weren't a couple—not yet—but they were very close friends." He looks at me. "Didn't he tell you? They bonded over their little siblings." Slowly, his voice calms as he recounts the details. "Laurent took care of me after our parents died, putting his own life on hold. And Emanuelle... From what I've heard, she stuck her neck out for her little sister. Natalie used to be... well, she'd gone off the rails. But Emanuelle never gave up on her. When her sister hit rock bottom—hospital visits and all—she nursed her back to health and took care of her. She got her a job at the opera and has been looking after her ever since."

Sébastien lets him talk as it seems to calm Théo down.

"Laurent and Emanuelle used to sit on the rafters together, taking each other's burdens off their shoulders. Not that I've been much of a burden lately, mind you, but I guess it was nice to be able to talk about these things with someone who really understood the kind of sacrifices they'd made."

"And Laurent developed feelings for her?" Sébastien asks quietly.

Théo nods. "He loved her. When I asked him why he didn't make a move, he said he didn't want to ruin their friendship, but then they slept with each other."

Sébastien frowns, and I know he's putting together a theory that fits Théo's account. If I had to guess, it doesn't look good for Laurent. "What was their relationship like afterwards? Did it change anything?"

"I don't know." Théo clicks his tongue, still struggling with his emotions. "They were busy performing Medée and rehearsing Castor et Pollux. There wasn't much time to redefine the relationship. I know Emanuelle wanted to take things slow, while Laurent was willing to give her time. But he was all in."

"Mhm. Was there anyone else? Was Emanuelle interested in someone else?"

Théo frowns as he catches on at last. "You think he did it. You think he was jealous because she rejected him or something." His voice gets angrier. "There was no one else. All Emanuelle cared about was her sister. They had an extremely close bond."

Sébastien looks at me as if he's asking for a second opinion. When I don't give him much, he turns to Théo with a sigh. "Look, from what you've told me, it seems Emanuelle was pretty busy with her sister and didn't have the time or energy to get involved with your brother. He might've been jealous of Natalie. That was her name, right?"

"Right," I say quietly.

But Théo groans. "Then why did he kill Emanuelle and not her?" He shakes his head angrily. "Someone planted this in his room. Maybe you're right. Maybe Natalie was jealous of *him* and decided she was the only one who could have her sister."

I can't imagine our friendly usher doing such a thing. But then I don't know her. Or Laurent. "What about Alexandra?"

Théo waves his arm at me. "Thank you! Everyone knew that Laurent and Emanuelle were close. Alexandra envied their bond. She could've killed her rival and then framed my brother."

Sébastien massages the bridge of his nose. "Are the dressing rooms under surveillance?" he asks suddenly.

"Not the rooms themselves, but the corridor."

"I'll check with management and see if I can get a copy of the security video. If someone set your brother up, they'll show up on camera."

Relief washes over Théo's face. "Yes. Yes!" Then he doubts himself again. "Can you do that? Can you really get a copy?"

"You'd be surprised what I can do." And with that, Sébastien leaves the room.

As soon as he's gone, Théo drops onto the nearest chair and buries his face in his hands. "My brother is not a murderer," he says, more to himself than to me.

I don't quite know what to do. Comfort him, yes, but how? I just wish Sébastien would hurry. As the minutes tick by, I take a deep breath and decide to pull myself together.

"It's going to be alright, Théo," I say as I walk over to him and put a hand gently on his shoulder.

Théo inhales sharply through his nose before looking up. "Thank you for coming so quickly. I didn't know who else to call."

A bitter smile flashes across his face. "That's the problem with not having any family."

I pull up a chair and sit down beside him. "Don't you have anyone?"

"We have a grandmother in the Pyrénées, but she's in her nineties. I can't possibly call her with news like this." He buries his head in his hands again, and I hear him sniffing. "I wish my parents were here."

Unable to bear so much misery, I put an arm around his shoulder and pull him to me. "They're not here, but I'm sure they're proud of you, Théo. Of Laurent, too."

"How would you know?" he cries. "You didn't even realise they were dead until last week."

"Because I've met their wonderful sons and seen the love they have for each other. That's the love your parents instilled in you." To be honest, I know because I've met countless dead parents watching over their children. Their love for their children never dies with them.

Théo leans a little closer to me. "I'm sorry I've been such an ass," he says after a while. "You're just... I had a crush on you when I first came to the Sorbonne, but you barely noticed me. Like I said, you're always in your own little world. You never really seemed to see me. Which is fine," he adds quickly. "You don't need to see me."

"Thanks?"

He laughs softly before saying, "You seem happy with Sébastien."

I don't know what to say. My heart's pounding like crazy, as if I've just been caught in a lie. *It's our good acting*, I tell myself. We've achieved what we set out to do. It's not real. But then why do I feel so guilty?

Fortunately, I don't have to answer as the door opens and Sébastien returns with a USB stick. "You have a computer?"

Théo pulls away from me and points to the workstation. "I'll log you on."

A few minutes later, the three of us are sitting in front of the computer, watching the video logs of the last two weeks. Even though Sébastien speeds up the videos, it's a tedious job. There are periods of activity, when people are constantly going in and out of their dressing rooms or visiting each other, and times when the corridor is just empty. Sometimes we see contemporary performers and sometimes it's one of the ghosts. Marie Pélissier is often seen using Emanuelle's dressing room, but Sébastien and I keep quiet about it. It's more likely she's claimed it for herself than anything else.

Théo quickly checks out, groaning in frustration. I also struggle with watching the videos. I don't even know what to look for, but Sébastien watches them carefully, rewinding and fast forwarding as he sees fit. He opens several windows and compares videos from different time stamps. At one point, Théo orders pizza.

"There!" Sébastien says, about two hours in. He's pulls up two windows next to each other. One's from Friday night, when the letters appeared on the door. The other's from a few hours later.

I gasp in shock. "It's Natalie."

In the video on the left, a hooded figure is painting big red letters on the door. The video on the right shows Natalie sneaking into Laurent's dressing room with the pot of paint and leaving without it. How could the police have missed this important piece of evidence?

"She wrote the note, yes, and here." Sébastien pulls up another video from two weeks ago. "That's her leaving Emanuelle's dressing room and going straight to where the costumes are kept."

Between us, Théo leans forward, his eyes narrowing in confusion. "What are you two talking about? I can't see anyone in these."

I meet Sébastien's eyes over Théo's head, an unspoken thought passing between us. The person on the video turns towards the camera and I see disfiguring scars all over her face. That's not Natalie. That's her whisper ghost.

CHAPTER 25

Well, crap! How do we get out of this? Sébastien and I see Natalie's ghost clearly, but Théo can't. He's not a ghost whisperer.

I rub my eyes for effect. "I think it's getting late. I'm starting to see things—"

"We have to go," Sébastien says, already standing up. He quickly closes the files and takes the flash drive.

"What do you mean you have to go?" Théo asks. "What about Natalie? What did you see?"

Sébastien puts the flash drive in his pocket. "That's classified information. I can't tell you anything."

"Class—what?" Théo looks at me for clarification.

I just shrug and follow Sébastien's lead. Obviously we're not going to try to hide anything and just rely on Sébastien's authority in this matter.

"Do you know where we can find Natalie at this hour?"

Angrily, Théo crosses his arms over his chest. "That's classified information."

Sébastien raises an eyebrow. "Really?"

"Private employee data. I can't reveal anything."

"Théo, please," I intervene. "Trust me, it'll help your brother."

He sighs heavily. "She lives in Via Claude Monet, but I doubt she's at home. Lately she's been spending all her time in Emanuelle's dressing room, grieving." Although he'd suggested it earlier, he now shakes his head. "She didn't kill her sister."

"She didn't," I tell him. According to what we've just seen on the security footage, her whisper ghost did.

As soon as we leave the room, I tell Sébastien, "I felt it. She felt like a ghost. Did she feel like a ghost to you?"

"I don't know," Sébastien confesses. "I was a bit distracted."

"By Voltaire," I remember.

Sébastien winces, as if he'd somehow let me down by not noticing she was a ghost whisperer. "Listen, when we talk to her, you have to let me take the lead. It's fine if you tell her you used to see ghosts too, but..."

"I can't let her know that I'm like her."

He nods and some of the tension leaves him. "Exactly. I've never seen her at GoPol, but that doesn't mean she's not one of our field agents."

I shudder at the thought of Voltaire's visit. Was it coincidence Natalie was our usher not once but twice? Or was she part of my surveillance? Was she listening to our conversation with Voltaire? Did she see how I handled myself in the dancers' foyer? Was that why C-Trente followed me to work?

We reach the corridor we've been watching on camera for hours. Emanuelle's dressing room door has been scrubbed clean, but I still see the faint outline of the letters. Behind the door I hear a faint sniffing.

Sébastien knocks politely. When there's no answer, he says, "Natalie, are you in there?"

A faint "Yes," comes in reply.

Cautiously, Sébastien opens the door and pokes his head into the room. "Bon soir. I know it's late, but we need to talk to you."

As I follow Sébastien into the dressing room, Natalie stares at us with bloodshot eyes. She sits in her sister's chair in front of the mirror and seems to be holding her breath. "What are *you* doing here?"

Someone else is standing behind her. It takes me a moment to recognise her in the jeans and blouse, but I've seen her picture enough on the news to be sure. It's Emanuelle Visse, the murdered soprano.

"We've never been formally introduced," says Sébastien. "Sébastien Roubert, GoPol agent." Then he nods at Emanuelle. "We meet again."

"You can see her?" Natalie asks in shock.

I close the door behind me and look down, not wanting to give away that I can see her, too.

"Indeed," Sébastien confirms. "I'm a bit surprised you can, though. When did your heart stop?"

"My heart?"

"He means have you ever been pronounced dead?" I say more quietly. "When did you start seeing ghosts?" Maybe I should just stay out of it, but I'm of the opinion that sympathy will serve us better than an interrogation.

Natalie inhales sharply. Her sister puts a hand on her shoulder and whispers, "It's alright, Nat. They're just here to help. Right?"

Sébastien nods at her.

Natalie takes a deep breath and I notice her fingers digging into her uniform. "Two years ago," she says at last. "I didn't know it was because of my injuries." She looks down at her fingers, clearly working through something. "I should have just died."

"No, you shouldn't." Emanuelle puts her arms around her sister. "I've told you that over and over again. You deserve a second chance."

When Natalie lifts her head, her eyes filled with tears. "But you would still be alive, Manu. You deserve that so much more than I do."

Emanuelle shakes her head. "That's not true. I don't deserve it any more than you."

"What happened?" I ask, wondering what happened between these two sisters who have so much love for each other, despite the fact one's whisper ghost allegedly murdered the other.

Natalie straightens her back and wipes her cheeks. "I got into a lot of trouble when I was younger. An abusive boyfriend, bad friends, drugs. I pushed anyone away who tried to help me. I said terrible things and did worse. Manu never gave up on me. My parents and brother did, but not Manu. She kept telling me how she'd be there for me. Of course, I didn't believe her. I *hated* her with a passion. Because she was... Mademoiselle Parfait, always shining like a goddamn star." The look she gives Emanuelle tells me the soprano's definitely her sister's star now.

"We lost touch for a while. I just couldn't stand being around her. She brought out all my insecurities, being so perfect while I was this huge mess. I was living in an abandoned building when Manu found me. She'd just gotten this job at the opera. I was high when she found me. Manu vowed to help me get clean and I tried. But it was so bloody hard. One day I found her going through my things. She'd found my stash and was going to throw it all in a bin. You know, one of those big industrial ones."

Natalie takes a few shaky breaths before continuing. "We had a fight. I said some really bad things. Like how I wanted her dead. And then she started a fire. She burnt my drugs." The memory makes her swallow and Emanuelle tightens her grip on her shoulder, tears on her own face. "And I went ballistic. I pushed her out of the way and dug through the fire, trying to salvage what I could, not even noticing it was burning my skin." She rolls up her sleeves and shows us some faint marks.

I remember the look on her ghost's face. Natalie has clearly had plastic surgery since then, but her ghost still wears those scars with pride. Just like the hatred.

"Manu tried to stop me. She got burnt too. I almost ruined her career," she says, as if that was the worst of it.

"No, you didn't. My injuries were minor."

Natalie shakes her head, clearly disagreeing. "I don't remember much, but Manu told me that I lost consciousness as she dragged me to safety. My heart stopped when they put me on a stretcher, but they brought me back quickly. I still had to be put in a medically induced coma for three weeks to give my injuries a chance to heal. When I woke up, I wanted to die. They'd already done some reconstructive work on my face, but I looked like a monster."

She looks up at her sister and smiles, finally returning the pressure of her hand. "Manu was there for me, every step of the way. She told me I was beautiful and slowly I started to look like it. I mean, it's not perfect, but that's just who I am, right?" She nervously rubs her scarred fingers.

"You're perfect to me," Emanuelle says with such warmth my heart aches. How nice would it be if Hélène thought I was perfect, despite all my imperfections?

"I didn't deserve her, but Manu is stubborn. She helped me with physiotherapy and getting clean. She moved me into her flat and got me a job. I owe her everything. And now I've killed her." She bursts into tears of guilt.

Sébastien squats down to her level before saying softly, "You didn't kill her. Your whisper ghost, that's what we call the remnant that stays behind, did."

"We?" Natalie asks.

"My own is a seventeen-year-old who can't take anything seriously and is always trying to stir up shit." Sébastien smiles affectionately. He really misses Dix. Then he nods at me. "Alix used to have a three-year-old, super sweet, and very expressive."

Natalie looks from him to me in awe. "You're like me?"

"I used to be."

"What does that mean?"

Sébastien sighs and slips back into his police routine. "There are ways to eliminate a whisper ghost. If they go rogue or cause harm."

"What harm has a three-year-old done?"

Yeah, I'd like to know that too, but all I can say is, "It's complicated."

"Alix can no longer see ghosts." Sébastien fixes Natalie with a stare. "We can take away your ghost, too."

My heart stops when he says these words. I know it's the GoPol way, and in this case, it probably has its merits, but I hate that it's so easy for him. To destroy an existence like that.

"Take her away?" Natalie asks, her eyes wide.

"She killed your sister, didn't she?"

Natalie swallows hard. "I think so. I met her a few weeks after I got the job at the opera. Manu had her first leading role. The opera was full of ghosts. It was overwhelming at first, but I really like them. They're a creative bunch of people, dramatic and full of passion, but they all come together to create art. Just like the living. My ghost is different. I try to stay as far away from her as possible. She's like all my worst sides rolled into one but made even more horrible".

"It happens," says Sébastien. "Sometimes, when people become whisperers, their whisper ghosts are created at the worst point in their lives. Whisper ghosts don't grow out of it, they don't evolve. Alix's was three for twenty years. In your case, your whisper ghost carries all the hate you felt at that moment. It turned her into—"

"A monster," Natalie whispers.

But I'm not thinking of Natalie's ghost when she says monster. Instead, my thoughts are with C-Trente. Now there's a real monster. Created at a point in Charles Roubert's life when he was cold and cruel. Not that he's changed much since then, but if anything, his whisper ghost is a true reflection of his depravity. He's Charles' monster to send out to do his dirty work.

"So can you take the other one away?" Emanuelle asks. "I'm not asking for justice for myself or anything, I just want my sister to be safe."

"Killing Natalie would end her existence," Sébastien explains.

"But does she know that?" Emanuelle asks. "My sister... she wasn't sane when she collapsed. I mean, she jumped into a burning trash can. If her whisper ghost is of that mind, she could try anything."

Natalie puts her hand on Emanuelle's, a new determination shining in her eyes. "If you can take her out, you have my blessing. Not because of me, but because I don't want her to hurt anyone else. There have been too many accidents, too much damage, and too many near misses. Who says she'll be satisfied now she's killed Manu? Please. Take her out."

Sébastien stands and nods. "We will. But first we have to find her."

"I know..." Natalie takes a deep breath. "I can take you to her hideout. The entrance is right here behind Manu's mirror."

Then she stands and reaches across the dressing table towards the gold frame of the mirror. She must've pressed something, because suddenly the mirror swings backwards. It's not quite the revolving door from the Phantom of the Opera, but it's a secret door all the same.

Sébastien looks at me. "You can stay here if you like."

"I'm coming with you." There's no way I'm letting him go alone. I understand that something has to be done about Natalie's ghost, but I'm not convinced elimination is the way to go. To me, her ghostly self has been through something traumatic—without a caring sister at her side. I don't agree with Sébastien that whisper ghosts don't evolve. Dix is the perfect example of that. He wanted so much more out of his existence than what he was. And even real ghosts evolve. Take my Panthéon ghosts. Perhaps, with love and understanding, we can heal this ghost's wounds instead of just making her disappear.

Suddenly something hits my back and I'm pushed forward. Panting, I turn to see the open door. Théo is standing there, eyes wide open. "If you're going, I'm going."

CHAPTER 26

"Théo!" I can't believe he's here. Has he been standing outside the door all this time?

His eyes sweep the room, skipping over Emanuelle before landing on Natalie. "My brother was arrested for this. You or your ghost or whatever is going on is framing him. So I'm coming with you." He looks into the hollow of the mirror and swallows. "Through there."

Sébastien moans. "On one condition."

Surprised, I look at him. "What?" Why are we letting Théo come?

"I want you to swear here and now that you won't tell anyone about this. Not even Laurent."

"Will you get him released?" Théo asks, his voice firm.

Sébastien nods sharply. "I'll get him released. You have my word." His eyes flick to me and I suddenly realise this condition is for my benefit. I'll still keep up my pretence, but if I slip, Théo won't blab.

"Then you've got mine," he says.

"Good," says Sébastien. "Then let's go." He swings his arm towards the opening, nodding at Natalie. "You'll have to lead us."

Natalie hasn't said a word since Théo burst into the room. Now she looks at him with renewed interest. "You knew about the ghosts?"

Théo cracks and laughs briefly. "I had no idea." His eyes meet mine and the sinking feeling in my stomach gets worse. There's no way tonight will be the end of it for him and me. All I can do is hope he takes Sébastien seriously and keeps his mouth shut.

One by one, we climb through the mirror into a dark passage. Once inside, Natalie closes the door before showing Sébastien the mechanism for opening it from the inside. She shines the flashlight on her phone to the left. "If you go that way, you'll come to a ladder that'll eventually lead you to the rafters. You can get out from there. I think it was used to make a surprise appearance on stage."

If so, the tunnel hasn't seen a performer for a long time. As we follow it to the right, our feet drag through decades of dust. It's also dark and narrow. Not much different from the catacombs. The walls are made of wood and stone, and here and there is a hole that allows someone in the tunnel to spy on those behind the walls.

I have no problem in this kind of place, but Théo keeps tugging at his collar as if he can't breathe. He must already be regretting his decision.

"It's okay," I tell him, stroking his arm gently. "There's enough air for all of us. Can you feel the breeze?" There's a draft just above our heads.

When he shakes his head, clearly not even trying, I take his hand and hold it in the air. "There."

It takes a few moments, but when he feels it, an audible wave of relief washes over him. "I can feel it."

"Good. Concentrate on that."

"I've never liked confined spaces," he confesses.

"Neither does Gaby. She'd never crawl into a hole in the wall." Unless someone she cared about was in danger.

Théo gives me a ghostly smile. "You seem fine."

"I wasn't fine on the rafters," I point out emphatically.

"I saw that." Slowly, Théo relaxes. "So... ghosts?" And there it is, the moment I was afraid of. "You can see ghosts?"

With a snort, I drop my arm again. "I can't... anymore."

"Why? What happened?" Before I can answer, he reveals exactly how long he's been listening at the door. "Someone took your ghost away."

I can't help it and cluck my tongue in frustration. "Yes. Someone."

Théo looks from me to Sébastien. "Did he?"

"Oh no, not him." Although at some point that was definitely his intention. I wave him off. "It's complicated. Classified information or something." It's most definitely on a need-to-know basis.

"I see. But that's what it is, isn't it? You can see ghosts. That's why you're so obsessed with the dignity of the dead in class, and why you always seem to be in your own world. Because you literally are." Judging by his tone, he seems neither shocked nor in awe, just like someone who's finally solved a puzzle and found the success not nearly as satisfying as he'd hoped. "So, what exactly are ghosts? Does everyone have one? Are they all evil?"

At the front, Emanuelle has her hand in Natalie's and speaks to her quietly.

"Of course not. They're people like us," I say.

At the same time, Sébastien looks over his shoulder and says: "There's a ghost with us, right here. Natalie's sister. If you could see her, you'd see a caring older sister who's only concerned about her sibling's safety".

Théo tries to catch a glimpse of her, but of course he's as blind as I'm supposed to be. "So everyone has one?"

"Yes. As long as people are remembered, their ghosts remain." Since he brought it up, I decide to finally clear something up. "That's what makes the catacombs so despicable. The ghosts they moved were already mostly forgotten, but by arranging them in this supposedly orderly fashion, they brought them back to existence. Only now they can't remember which leg or head belonged to them." After all these months, the memory still tastes like acid.

Théo's eyes widen. "That's why you kept going on and on about the catacombs. It all makes sense now."

"So you agree?"

"Well, I'd probably have to see it myself or at least learn a bit more about ghosts and think about it, but I see your point, okay?"

It's not a victory, but it's pretty close. Something inside me heals and my smile for Théo comes much easier.

When I turn my gaze back to the front, I find Sébastien watching me, unspoken questions written on his face. I'd never told him about the situation in the catacombs. Maybe when this is over, we can visit them together and brainstorm how to solve the ghosts' dilemma—after we deal with GoPol, of course.

We've reached the end of the tunnel and find a winding staircase that takes us deeper into the Opera. If I remember correctly, the Opera has seventeen floors above ground and five below. Plus a secret entrance to the real catacombs. Judging by where we started, we're close to the ground floor now.

"So if you can see everyone who's still remembered, you must see a lot of historical people, don't you?" Théo is definitely too smart for his own good. "And you work in the Panthéon." He laughs softly. "That's cheating, Alix."

I roll my eyes. "It's not cheating. They could tell me the sky was green back then and I'd still have to find a proper source. But it helps to understand some of the conflicts."

"So you really know them? Curie, Dumas, Moulin, Voltaire?" Théo asks, now sounding in awe.

"Remember when we went to the Panthéon in second year?" When he nods, I grin. "That's when I met Victor Hugo."

"No way! That was..." He laughs again. "No wonder I never had a shot. I mean, I'd have picked Hugo too."

Now I'm the one laughing. Théo understands how cool it is to hang out with all these people. It's almost a shame thinking we could've had this kind of relationship for years if only I'd trusted him. But it took me over a year to confess to Gaby, and even she needed solid proof before she believed me.

He sobers up as we descend another level. "So everyone turns into a ghost when they die?"

"Pretty much."

"And then they do what? Just float around?"

"Well, the ghosts in the opera put on shows. Voltaire and Rousseau continue their feud. Hugo, Dumas, and Zola are always discussing new story ideas. Most ghosts enjoy the same things they did in life. Or they hang out in the cemeteries and... they date."

Théo looks at me incredulously. "They date?"

Surprisingly, I'm not thinking of Gaspar. "My grandmother, Estelle, has finally started dating Alexandre de Beauharnais, you know, Josephine's ex-husband."

"Napoleon's Josephine?"

"That's the one." The good thing when talking to history students is you don't have to explain your references. "He's been courting her for years and she's finally given in."

"Your dead grandma is dating a revolutionary general?" He snorts in disbelief, but the amusement doesn't last long. "So you're able to talk to someone? Anyone who's dead?"

"I—"

"Like my parents?"

My heart breaks a little. He asks in such an uncertain way, as if he's already bracing for my answer. The worst thing is that I absolutely could, but I can't admit it. "Not anymore," I lie quietly. I've never felt so bad about the lie that keeps me alive as I do now.

Théo snaps out of it. "Right, I forgot. You lost your powers." Not surprisingly, his eyes drift to Sébastien.

I'm convinced Sébastien's heard every single word. He must feel those eyes burning in the back of his head. But he doesn't offer and Théo doesn't ask. Reconnecting loved ones is not part of GoPol's standard training.

"Down here," Natalie says quietly. She's pushed a box out of the way, revealing a trapdoor in the floor. "I've never been down there." She hugs herself. "It scares me so much."

"We've got it from here," says Sébastien. He wastes no time in sitting down on the edge of the hole and letting himself fall in. From the sound of it, he lands easily. "It's only two metres."

Théo follows his example, although he looks a little more cautious and takes a deep breath before jumping in.

I'm about to go next when I suddenly hear EDM music behind me, not in front. Unable to resist the sound, I look over my shoulder.

"You hear it, don't you?" Natalie says quietly. "The Angel of Music is calling you."

I swallow hard. "Why? Who are they?" Not a ghost, apparently, because Théo heard the music too.

Slowly I walk towards the music, away from the trapdoor. Natalie follows me. "He," she corrects me. "He made me send the ghost. Made me buy the tickets. He wants you. Said you're his muse."

Suddenly I don't feel so good. The person behind the music really wants *me*. Natalie knows the mysterious man behind the music and she's been instrumental in getting me here? "But I thought your whisper ghost—"

"They're not the same."

Just as she says that, I hear a terrible sliding sound, like stone sliding over stone. I whirl towards the trapdoor, which is now closed. On it stands a woman who, apart from the ruin of her face, looks exactly like the one next to me.

"You should've been down there," she says, a manic gleam in her eyes. "Oh well. The show must go on."

As if on cue, Sébastien and Théo start shouting my name.

CHAPTER 27

M y eyes can't decide what to look at. The woman with the
gruesome burn marks on her face and hands, the trap
door, or Natalie. My heart pounds in my chest as I hear Sébastien
and Théo calling for help. What's happening? What's she doing to
them?

"Alix!" Sébastien cries out in a strained voice. "Alix, open the
door! Quick!"

His desperation tears me apart. My heart drops like a stone into
my stomach as I remember the Phantom's torture chamber. After
Christine was kidnapped, Raoul and the Persian tried to break into
his house, but they ended up in a torture chamber instead. Using a
combination of mirrors, sounds, images, and heat, he slowly drove
them mad. They would've killed themselves if Christine hadn't
saved them.

Now I'm the one on the outside, and I have no idea how to help them, because one thing's for sure, this woman's not madly in love with me like the Phantom was with Christine.

"You can't see ghosts, can you?" she says in a singsong voice. Then she comes towards me. Her creepy smile, which only moves one part of her face, gets wider and wider. Since I'm staring at her the whole time, the question is pretty moot, but she already knew that. "How about—?"

Just before she reaches me, Natalie slides in front of me. "Don't touch her! She's done nothing to you."

"I heard them talking. Her and the tall one. They want to *eliminate* me. They're from the ghost police." Her voice falls dangerously low. "We don't like those pigs."

Me and you both, sister. "I'm not," I say, suddenly feeling a little more capable. This is a ghost formed by hatred and despair, not a broken tool to be replaced. "I'm not the police. In fact, they're after me too."

If I was hoping for sympathy, I'm sorely disappointed. Junkie Nat just cackles. "What have you done? Run off with that pretty agent? I don't think you're telling the truth. You know what I think?" She pauses for a heartbeat before happily proclaiming, "You're a *liar*. You tell people you lost it, but I know you can see me, hear me, *feel* me." She leaps over Natalie's shoulder so suddenly I jump.

Luckily Natalie anticipated it and grabs her before she can touch me. "Don't! You can't go around killing people. Let them go. Please. I don't want this."

Junkie Nat turns her attention to Natalie. "When was the last time you cared about what *I* want?"

"What do you want?" I ask before Natalie can answer, still trying to get through to her.

Junkie Nat holds back for a minute, pondering my question. Then her eyes light up. "I want to see the whole world... *burn*. Let them all burn. It'll be glorious."

Yeah, maybe Sébastien got this one right.

She claps her hands. "Let's burn something now." Her eyes meet mine. "Or someone."

"No!" I try to stop her, but Natalie is in the way and we both fall to the floor instead. These corridors are too damn narrow.

Meanwhile, Junkie Nat skips back to the trapdoor and picks up something from the floor. Concealed by the shadows, I didn't see the long, thin rope. No, not a rope, a fuse, and Junkie Nat is lighting a match. "Let's make something explode."

Natalie scrambles up and rushes her, but it's too late, the fuse is lit.

As Natalie and her evil alter-ego crash into the crates that used to cover the trapdoor, I try to stomp the fuse out. But no matter how many times I trample on it, it just keeps on burning. When I realise it won't work, I throw myself into the dirt above the trapdoor. "Sébastien!" I call in desperation.

He's not screaming any more, but I hear muffled groans. Whatever's happening down there is quickly draining their strength.

"Séb!" I shout again.

"Alix?" the answer is tired and weak, much too weak. Then he bangs against the wall. "Open the door."

Good idea. Why didn't I think of that? I push up on my knees and try to find a handle. There isn't one. How did Natalie open it before? I push and pull, hammer and kick. Nothing. Meanwhile, the lit end of the fuse is getting closer and closer.

"I can't do it! You... you have to..." *Breathe, Alix. Think about what you need to say to him.* "Do you see a fuse?"

"A fuse?" Under the door, I hear him breathing heavily. "Shit, Alix! This room is full of gas."

Suddenly my hand is on the small piece of fuse that hasn't burned yet. "I'll pull it out!" Immediately I jump up and pull with all my weight. The fuse moves about an arm's length, then stops. I wrap it around my hand once more to get away from the fire and pull again. It's like pulling on a rock. "It's stuck." It must be attached to something.

"I know!" Sébastien calls from below. "I've got a knife."

Nervously, I watch the red glow coming closer and closer to my hand and the trapdoor. "Hurry!"

I feel him cutting from the tension in my hands, but he's weak and his breathing is heavy. He's already been under the influence of the gas for too long. What kind of gas, I have no idea.

Despite the weight, I try to pull again. The heat's getting closer.

"Come on!" I grunt.

Then the burning end reaches me, and I almost let go of the fuse when the sharp pain of heat sears my skin. "Sébastien!" It'll only take thirty seconds for the fuse to burn through the length of my hand and then... and then it'll hit the room full of gas and there'll be two more ghosts in my life.

Tears run down my cheeks from sheer exhaustion. My hand aches, the fire eating away at my flesh. Then suddenly something snaps, and I fall backwards with the rest of the rope.

The knife. Sébastien did it. It takes me another second to realise this means I can let go of the fuse. As soon as I do, I hiss in pain. I can't see the angry red mark in the dark, but I know I've just burnt the side of my hand. The rest of the rope has left deep indentations, maybe even cuts in my skin. It hurts like hell.

But it'll have to wait. I stopped the explosion, but they're still trapped in a room full of gas. Maybe poison gas. I remember how weak Sébastien sounded, and I haven't heard from Théo in a while.

Natalie's still fighting her whisper ghost. They bump into old, dusty sets and roll around the storage space. Emanuelle tries to help, but she's never been particularly scrappy. From what I can see, it won't be long before Junkie Nat gets the upper hand.

Ignoring the pain in my hand, I grab my phone and try to figure out this trapdoor. "Sébastien? Are you still there?"

"They're everywhere," I hear him groan. "There are bugs everywhere. I have to get out."

Are there really bugs in the room below or is he hallucinating? Neither option bodes well for him. "And Théo?"

If I strain my ears hard enough, I think I hear a second moan.

"Get me out!" Sébastien shouts, clearly panicking.

"I'm working on it," I promise, panic eating away at me too. I can't lose him. Not like this. Once more I run my hands over the trapdoor. How did Natalie open it before?

Then I remember. She didn't. It was a hole in the ground, covered by a large crate. Now it's a square of smooth stone that looks like an ordinary floor tile. There's no handle, no pressure point, but there must be a mechanism.

What if Sébastien dies while I'm trying to figure this out? The thought almost takes my breath away.

"Garnier!" If anyone can help me solve this, it's the architect of the building. "Garnier!" I don't have a close relationship with him, but he asked for my help, so this is the least I can do.

Just as I'm about to call a third time, he appears. "What is it?" He finds me kneeling on the floor. "Mademoiselle Dubois?"

"I need your help. There are two people trapped in a room full of gas. How do I open this?"

He looks nervously over his shoulder where Junkie Nat has Natalie pinned against the wall. I should probably help her, but I can't leave Sébastien and Théo alone. Not when they could soon be dead.

"Is that...?" he asks, sounding as if he's about to bolt.

"You promised your help!" I snap. "Everyone's help!"

Garnier drops down beside me. "The opera has many secrets, thanks to that damned phantom."

Just then, others arrive. It only takes me one glance to realise they're all ghosts. The tunnel doesn't allow for many of them, and for a moment I panic that they're going to crowd me so much I won't be able to move at all, but then a stagehand shouts from a little further ahead. "There's something here."

I push past Garnier to where the stagehand is and find a small lever in the corner of a support beam and wall that I would never have found. As soon as I pull the lever, the trapdoor opens.

A second later I'm hit by a cloud of sweet-smelling gas. I try to hold my breath, but my throat's already tingling and I swear I can feel the legs of a thousand bugs on my skin. Worst of all, I'm about to lose consciousness.

CHAPTER 28

When my head clears and the tingling subsides, I'm lying propped up against a wall a few metres down the corridor. Did I crawl here? Did someone move me?

I blink and look into Marie Pélissier's eyes. "She's alive!"

"Of course she's alive, you imbecile!" Le Maure snorts. "If she wasn't, she'd be a ghost by now."

That's a good point. And since I can't see a second me, I can safely assume my heart hasn't stopped, either. Still, my head is spinning, and I feel like throwing up. Whatever gas Junkie Nat has down there is nasty.

Speaking of gas, Sébastien and Théo need my help! I jump to my feet, desperate to find the trapdoor. The ghost who dragged me away didn't drop me that far, and I can see the open rectangle in front of me. A few ghosts are standing around it, seemingly invested in what lies below.

When I finally manage to look down, I see Sébastien and Théo on the ground. Théo is groaning, while Sébastien's sitting up with the help of Garnier. They're alive.

A massive sigh of relief escapes me as I sit back and allow myself to relax for a moment. But not for long. Then I remember Natalie and her whisper ghost.

Once again, I look around wildly, made more difficult by the number of ghosts around me. The two of them have made a huge mess of the tunnel. Everywhere I look I see rubble and splinters of wood.

"If you're looking for the monster," Le Maure says, "she's down there."

I stumble in the direction she points, until I come upon a scene so horrifying I forget to breathe. Natalie is lying on the floor, bleeding from a head wound and many others. While her sister sits by her side in tears, her whisper ghost crouches over her, poking her like a child poking a dead animal with a stick. Since it's still there, I assume Natalie is alive. But for how long?

"If she dies, at least that'll be the end of this monster," says Pélissier with a certain smugness. "Have you seen her face?"

Up close, it's hideous, no question, but I don't see a monster. I see a tragedy, a life snatched away so young, leaving nothing but pain and hatred.

"It's appalling," Le Maure agrees. "Even worse than him."

"Shut up!" I bark at the two divas. "You're not helping."

They both turn their noses up at me, and for a moment I'm afraid their entire fan clubs are going to turn on me. Fortunately, there's not enough room for that.

When I turn to look at Natalie, I catch Emanuelle's gaze instead. "Please. This is all my fault. If I hadn't started the fire—"

"I'd still be alive!" Junkie Nat hisses, her eyes gleaming again.

Someone snorts behind me. "As if."

I've had enough of this. One word from me and I could probably send the ghosts behind me into action. They'd tear Junkie Nat away from Natalie and allow me to get her help. But that would only send her further down this spiral of hatred, and who knows what her anger would do. She may very well bring down the whole opera house.

Instead, I approach her cautiously, like a wounded animal. "Are you okay?" Not the most intuitive question, but I hope it's the one that'll serve me best.

"She should've died a long time ago," says Junkie Nat, not taking her eyes off the sprawled body.

"I know. Two years ago."

"But she didn't. *I* did."

I recognise this bitterness from Dix. Sébastien was brought back to life, but he left a part of himself behind. Now separated, Dix had many feelings about his death. "It's not fair."

"No, it's not." Junkie Nat's burning eyes meet mine as she turns to me. "It's not fair she gets to live a comfortable life with my sister and every ghost fawning over her, while I'm down here alone, hated by them all." She throws the divas a withering look.

Flustered, they hide behind fans and whisper to each other. I hear the words "phantom", "crazy", and "capricious" coming out of their mouths. Again, it doesn't help.

Instead of telling the divas to leave us alone, I concentrate on Junkie Nat. I really should stop calling her that. She's so much more than all her failures and pain put together. "What happened to you wasn't fair," I say.

Following an instinct, I place a hand gently on her cheek. It feels rubbery. The skin is too tight and deeply scarred. "Nobody should've died that day, but bad things happen in this world."

"They always happen to me," Nat says bitterly.

"Evil reaps what evil sows," Le Maure whispers.

I almost explode. "Don't listen to them. You're not evil and you're not a monster." That term's reserved for real monsters like Charles Roubert and his whisper ghost. "You're just someone who needed help." All of this is just one big cry for help. "I'm here to help."

Out of the corner of my eye I see some of the more proactive ghosts sneaking in and dragging Natalie to safety. Since she's like me, they have no problem handling her. What surprises me more is Emanuelle staying where she is, watching us.

"You know death isn't the end," I continue. "In a way, it's a new beginning, a fresh start."

"If anything, it's worse!" Nat hisses, almost making me recoil. "These ghosts are just as bad as the living. Judgemental, the whole lot of them."

Pélissier and Le Maure immediately take the bait. "She's a murderer! A lunatic. Unnatural!"

Nat's eyes burn and I feel the air charge. I put both my hands on her face, forcing her to stay with me. "Look at me, Nat."

At the same time, Emanuelle jumps to her feet. "Don't talk like that about my sister! She's done nothing to you."

My heart explodes with warmth at her words. That's sisterhood for you.

It's a shame Pélissier and Le Maure have nothing better to do with their afterlife than compete with each other and look down on others. They probably contributed a lot to Nat's descent into madness by confusing her with their stupid phantom stories. And Nat, in turn, contributed to their increased conflict. A vicious circle; deadly even.

"Ignore them. They don't deserve your attention. They only care about themselves." As the divas huff and puff, something of the mad gleam in Nat's eyes fades. Maybe I'm finally getting through to her. "Look, you don't have to surround yourself with toxic people. Just because you're Natalie's whisper ghost doesn't mean you have to be around them. You're free, Nat, free to be whoever you want to be, wherever you want to be. You don't have to live your afterlife in the shadows."

Again, I'm reminded of Dix, who wanted nothing more than to be his own person. As much as it hurt Sébastien, going rogue may have been the freedom he always craved.

"I know many ghosts who are more than willing to help you. If you want, I can put you in touch with any of them."

"You want to introduce me to your friends?" Nat asks incredulously, as if no one,s been willing to do that for a long time.

"Of course. I've helped many ghosts before. I can help you." There are a few obstacles to this plan, but when has that ever stopped me?

I have Nat's full attention now. The other ghosts have faded away, either keeping quiet or deserting the place for lack of a dramatic showdown.

Nat raises her own hands and runs her fingers over my face. "You're pretty."

"So are you." I know she doesn't have to exist with the scars. She can change her appearance once she's able to move past this, but I won't suggest it. It's not our looks that make us beautiful, it's our hearts.

"You want to be my friend?" Nat asks in wonder.

"Is that so hard to believe?" I tease her gently, knowing full well how hard it would be for her to trust me after all that animosity thrown at her.

But Nat smiles and this time it doesn't look so creepy. "Just making sure."

Her hands move down. Suddenly they're wrapped around my neck, squeezing. Shocked, my hands fly up to meet hers. "What are you... doing?" I croak, struggling for air.

"I'm making you my friend. We'll be together forever." The madness is back in her eyes. "We don't need others. It'll just be the two of us, down here. You'll look after me. That's what you do, don't you?"

How could I have got this so wrong?

"Don't..." The pressure in my throat only increases. My lungs are screaming for air. I try not to panic, but there's little reason not to. It doesn't seem like anything's getting through to her. "Please."

Nat pushes down on me and giggles happily. "We're going to have so much fun together."

Music fills my ears. Is it him? Is my Angel of Music coming to rescue me? Or was this his plan all along?

Someone yanks me out of Nat's grip and pulls me back as others descend on her, calling her every foul name in the book. Nat snarls and kicks, while it takes four men to pull her away from me. Music swells, suffocating the small space.

I can't breathe. Even though the grip on my throat is gone, I struggle to fill my lungs with air. There's too much chaos, too much anger and drama. I'm drowning all over again.

"Stop!" Emanuelle's command cracks like a whip through the tunnel. "Let go of my sister right now!"

Tiny, slender Emanuelle certainly has a set of pipes on her. Her voice fills the whole tunnel and makes all the other ghosts stop what they are doing. Even Nat.

Emanuelle glares at the men holding her. "Now!"

All four drop Nat like a hot potato. The whisper ghost looks like a feral beast, absolutely terrified of the crowd around her.

"Everyone leave," I hear myself say.

"You belong with us, Emanuelle Visse," says Pélissier. "With me."

"Who says she wants to be with you?" Le Maure asks, ready to start the fight again.

Emanuelle ignores them both and kneels before Nat instead. "Ignore them. I would choose you over any of them."

The divas snort at this and finally ease up. As they gather up their skirts and make their way out of the tunnel, the tension drops dramatically. I can finally breathe again.

"I killed you," Nat says to her sister in disbelief. "Why would you want anything to do with me?"

"Because I'm your sister, Nat. I love you. Even if you don't love yourself." With big sad eyes, Emanuelle cocks her head. "It's my fault you died that day. Don't you think I haven't beaten myself up about it every day? If only I hadn't thrown them away. If only I hadn't lit that fire. It's only fair you took your revenge on me."

It's not fair at all. Emanuelle tried to help her sister and a terrible tragedy occurred. That doesn't excuse murder. But I keep my mouth shut and let her do her thing. In a way, it's comforting to see a sister's love endure.

"Nat, all I ever wanted was for you to be safe and happy," Emanuelle continues. "It hurts me that *I* was the cause of so much pain for you. I didn't know what was happening, that you existed in so much misery. I didn't see you. But I see you now. We can be together now, far away from the opera, if that's what you want."

I can see why everyone loved Emanuelle. She's the sweetest, kindest person I've ever met. Even though her sister's ghost took her life, she's ready to forgive, to heal, and to move on.

Emanuelle puts her hands on Nat's face and kisses her forehead. "You and me, Nat. Just like when we were children. I won't leave you again. I'll be with you to the end."

Nat starts to cry. She falls into her sister's arms and hugs her as if she'll never let her go again. "I promise to be better. I'll try. I'll make it this time."

Emanuelle's smile spreads all over her face. "Of course you will. I believe in you."

My heart yearns for what they share. Beneath all those misunderstandings, the hate, and the desperation, is a pair of sisters who love each other. And I get it. I get it so much it hurts. We may hate each other sometimes, but in the end we're still sisters.

In the end, Nat doesn't get the chance to do better. After waking up and managing to make his way out of the hole with the help of some ghosts, Sébastien arrests the whisper ghost. He doesn't do it unkindly, and my throat hurts too much to stop him. If the last hour has taught me anything, it's that Nat is too unstable. She may have a chance with Emanuelle by her side, but the risk is too great. And in this world, the living still take precedence over the dead.

I hate it. I wish there was some kind of ghost therapy instead, some kind of rehabilitation programme like in the real world. Instead, GoPol wins again. Their methods are tried and tested.

Two agents pick Nat up from the foyer as paramedics attend to my hand and to Natalie, who is awake and alert. "What's happening now?" she asks Sébastien, watching as her whisper ghost is led outside, Emanuelle at her side. At least the ghost is keeping her promise.

"GoPol has ways of ending her existence. When that happens, you'll no longer be able to see ghosts."

Natalie swallows. "Never again?"

"Well, unless you have another accident, which I can't really recommend."

She chuckles softly. "No, that doesn't sound desirable." Then she sighs. "I'm going to miss this place."

"You won't lose your job," says Sébastien, confused.

"But everything else. All the magic. Pélissier and Le Maure fighting."

From upstairs I hear the two of them at it again. Now they're fighting about whose fault it is Emanuelle is joining neither side.

Natalie rolls her eyes at me. "I'm with Voltaire. Pélissier for the art. Le Maure for the voice."

I can't help laughing. The sopranos won't be happy about this, but they'll continue their rivalry for another hundred years. Hopefully without any murders.

Natalie's eyes land on the door through which the GoPol agents, her whisper ghost, and her sister have disappeared. "I wish I could say goodbye to my sister."

"You can call her here. I'm sure she'd listen to you."

Natalie shakes her head quickly. "Oh no. I had her for two good years. The other part of me needs her more than I do." She smiles bravely. "And she's not leaving me, right? She'll always be there, watching over me."

Now that my hand's bandaged up, I put it on hers. "You can be sure of that."

"I'll make her proud," Natalie says with fierce determination. "I won't waste this second chance. Never."

The paramedics insist they have to go now, and Sébastien and I take a step back to where Théo sits on the Grand Staircase, watching the proceedings with an exhausted expression. He looks like someone who's bitten off more than he can chew.

"GoPol will clear the case with the police," Sébastien tells him. "Your brother should be released tomorrow morning."

Théo looks up gratefully. "Thank you." Then his eyes meet mine. "You talked the ghost down."

"No, Emanuelle—" The words sink in and I realise what he's just said. He and Sébastien must have woken up much earlier than I'd thought.

Sébastien noticed it, too. "Théo, this is very important. If you care about Alix, keep this to yourself. Don't tell anyone what you saw or heard."

I hold my breath as Théo considers the request. At last, he nods. "I told you, you have my word. If my brother asks tomorrow, I'll just tell him you found who did it. I wasn't there. He doesn't need to worry about me hunting down murderers anyway."

"Thank you," I say, genuinely grateful. "And yes, we can visit your parents."

"Alix," Sébastien warns.

"They're in Lyon. Far away from here." What I don't say is that I'm through with hiding. I'm not going to announce to the world that I can see ghosts again or anything like that, but I'm not going to refuse the dead when they come to me for help. Often, I'm all they have, and I can't live my life with regret or ignore their pain.

Speaking of regret, it's time to visit my sister.

CHAPTER 29

After a good night's sleep, I call on my sister. I know there's a risk Cédric will be there, but I'm willing to take it. My sister loves him, and although I'll never forgive him, he's just another victim of Charles Roubert's. That's how I intend to see him. It's the best I can do.

Hélène is already home from work, as I knew she'd be. She's still in her business attire when she opens the door for me. "Alix?" I'm probably the last person she expected to see.

"Can I come in?"

I don't know if it's my calm question or her own sense of propriety that makes her reconsider slamming the door in my face, but she sighs and takes a step back. "Of course."

Though I still carry a lot of resentment, I force it down and say, "I came to apologise."

Her tense expression betrays how much she wants to throw the words back in my face. "Let's sit down."

To my great relief, Cédric isn't home yet, so it's just me and Hélène. She leads me into her living room and we both sit on the couch. There's no offer of a drink or anything.

"Did Maman send you?" Hélène asks cautiously.

I shake my head. "No one sent me. I came because... you're my sister." Seeing Natalie and Emanuelle yesterday drove that point home. I may not like Hélène's choice of husband, but I don't want her to hate me as much as Natalie once hated Emanuelle. And I certainly don't want to be the one who hates her.

Hélène clicks her tongue, still cautious. "You said I wasn't."

"I was hurt. You always had my back when we were younger, and now it feels like you've turned against me."

"Alix, *you*—"

"I know!" I cut her off quickly, before we can start arguing instead of apologising. "It's not for me to question your relationship. But I was just looking out for you."

"You don't have to look out for me," Hélène protests.

"But that's what sisters do." I inhale deeply and take her hands in mine. "That's what you did. I didn't ask you to, but you always looked out for me. You didn't know the ghosts were real and you just wanted to make sure I was okay. And yes, lately I've gotten into a lot of trouble because of my abilities, but it's not because I'm stupid or wilful or—"

"It's because you care too much," Hélène says, her voice finally softening. "I'm sorry I didn't believe you."

Warmth spreads through my chest as she finally admits how she let me down. I trusted her with everything. And then she moved on without me, got her own life, and threw me away like an unwanted piece of her past. I don't hate Hélène, but I understand where Nat's anger comes from.

"It didn't sound very credible."

"No, it didn't." Hélène laughs, and just like that the ice is broken and her shoulders relax. "I mean, come on. How am I supposed to believe Paris is full of dead people who are just going on with their afterlives?"

You could've trusted me. I push the unhelpful thought aside and laugh with her. "I know it's a lot to ask, but you should know that I'd never lie to you."

Not about the important stuff. At least, until recently.

If Hélène gets the hint, she ignores it. She turns her hands around so she can hold mine properly. In the process, she notices the Band-Aid on my hand. "What's that?"

"I played with fire. The fire won."

Her face falls in concern. "I thought you'd lost your ability."

"What? You think I need ghosts to get into trouble?" And there goes my "don't lie to my sister" policy.

She laughs, believing me at once. "Oh, Alix. You know, Maman and Papa think Odi is the wild child, but it's always been you. On the outside, you seem so calm and sweet. Inside, you're burning with passion." She sighs, as if resigned. "But why choose ghosts? You're such an intelligent girl. You could have so many friends."

"I do. I mean, I used to." It's hard to talk about this without getting into a fight. How do I make my sister understand? She already has all the facts, but she doesn't come to the same conclusion as I do. "Whispering is different. For me it wasn't ghosts and the living. They were all just people. And I just happened to get along better with ghosts than the living. They were real friends to me, very dear friends."

"Like Gaspar?" she asks, surprisingly softly.

Tears burn in my eyes. "I really loved him. He was sweet and caring. He loved music and dreamt of becoming a social worker. His parents weren't a big fan of that, but he wanted to help those who didn't have a loud voice."

"What happened? I mean… how did he die?"

"Road accident. He was on his bike." I don't tell her how I met him at the site of his accident. "But death didn't change him. He still loved this world… and me. He even got on well with Malou," I add.

Hélène looks at me with sad eyes. "I'm sorry, Alix. He sounds like a good guy. I wish you'd met him when he was alive. When I could've seen him."

"Me, too." Before the sadness overwhelms me, I shake it off and take a deep breath. "I wish he was still here, too, but he's gone and I... Sébastien isn't so bad, either."

"Well..." Hélène grimaces and scoffs.

Quickly, I squeeze her hands. "I know, I know, he and Cédric don't see eye to eye. But from what I've heard, neither of them had the best childhood. Sébastien grew up as an only child, without a mother. His father always pushed him to be the best. Even if it meant showing up his cousin. It's hard to break those patterns, and I bet Cédric wasn't *always* playing nice either."

With a shake of her head, Hélène concedes, "Probably not. He has a *bit* of an inferiority complex which I've never really understood. That's why I'm so happy he finally got the job he wanted."

Oh, yes, the job he got by ratting me out. "Well, maybe working together will be good for them." I really hope not. "You know, they just need to work out their own shit. We don't have to get involved."

Hélène grins mischievously. "No, we don't." She changes her grip so that she's holding one of my hands with both of hers. "Let's make a promise, okay? We won't let any boy drama come between us. If they've got a problem with each other, they'll have to sort it out themselves. We'll just sit back and drink champagne."

If only it were that easy. Nevertheless, I chuckle. "Sounds good to me. Does that mean I can come to your wedding?"

"Are you okay with me marrying Cédric and will you be nice to him?"

I don't like it, but she's more important to me than my grudge against Cédric. "I can play nice. And if you love him and he makes you happy, then I'm happy for you." Just don't expect me to share more sensitive details about my life.

Hélène leans forward and pulls me into a hug. "Then yes, of course you can come."

My stomach hurts as I hold her. It feels like I've compromised too much, but one of us had to. It's the price I have to pay for my sister. She and Cédric are a package deal, even before they've signed a piece of paper. We don't have to be close, but I'm determined to at least be civil.

Hopefully, her future husband will show me the same courtesy.

CHAPTER 30

Two days later, Gaby, Malou, and I take the train to Lyon with Théo. Gaby insisted on coming because she didn't want me to go anywhere alone after hearing about C-Trente's visit to the Panthéon—and apparently because she wanted to lay down some ground rules for Théo.

"You can't tell anyone about this. You can't make fun of her. And you can't bother her. This is a one-off." She has her finger in his face, the tip coming closer and closer to his eyes as she makes point after point. I give Théo credit for barely flinching throughout. "And no strange love confessions. That ship has sailed. Move on."

Théo laughs when she finally lowers her finger. "She's happy with Sébastien. At first, I thought he was just some annoying jock with a motorbike, but he's actually cool. And they make a great team. Besides," he shrugs, "when you've been locked in a gas chamber together, there's something like a bro code."

"Great, good to know you need to be knocked upside the head a few times like all guys before you become a decent one."

When Théo pouts, I can't help but laugh. Gaby's simply the best.

Satisfied she's made her point, she sits next to me again. "You might think it's funny or cool," her voice is different now, much more serious than before, "but it's not. Alix's life is in danger if anyone finds out."

"Gaby, lay off!" Théo pleads. "I already promised Sébastien I'd keep the secret."

"Oh, well, if you promised another guy!" Gaby rolls her eyes.

"I'll promise you, too, if it's so important to you. Alix's secret is safe with me. I won't even tell my brother."

Gaby crosses her arms, but nods. "Very well, you've got my trust for now."

"Thank you," Théo says humbly and slightly amused. Then his gaze falls on me and I see the worry in it. "Your life's in danger? Is this trap endangering you?"

"No, it's—"

"Yes, it is," Gaby interrupts. "But Alix will do it anyway because she's that awesome."

I snort. "More like, Lyon is two hours from Paris, and we should be safe there."

"What's going on?" Théo asks. "Are the ghosts after you?"

It's far too early to tell him all about GoPol, so instead I leave it at, "Let's just say I dug a little too deep and pissed off some powerful people."

"Shit, Alix. Who?"

"Believe me, it's better I don't drag you into my mess. It's too dangerous."

Angrily, Théo crosses his arms over his chest and leans back. "More dangerous than a murderous whisper ghost in control of an ancient trap mechanism? Alix, I almost got blown up."

"You insisted on coming," I point out.

Suddenly he leans forward again. "And I want to come this time, too. Metaphorically speaking." He nods at Gaby. "I'm in. Whatever's going on, I'm in."

Gaby scoffs. "You don't even know what this is about. We're talking about government-level shit."

Théo's eyes widen a little. "Are we?" Then he snorts. "Well, it wouldn't be the first time the government got important things wrong. I trust Alix more than any of them, so count me in."

Gaby and I exchange glances and an unspoken conversation passes between us. Finally, Gaby takes Malou from me. "Swear it on Malou."

Théo looks a little sceptical. "On a hedgehog wearing a scarf?"

"She can sniff out ghosts better than anyone I know," I tell him.

"Swear it," Gaby demands again.

"Jeez, Gaby, calm down." Théo carefully puts his hands on Malou's spikes. "I swear on Malou and her fancy scarf that I'm all in. I will keep Alix's secrets and trust her judgement." He frowns. "Why does it feel like I just signed my life away?"

"Because if GoPol finds out, you might as well have."

He gasps. "GoPol? As in the ghost police? I thought your boyfriend was a GoPol agent..."

With a sigh, I begin to tell him the broad outlines of my conflict with GoPol. He already knows about whisper ghosts and their elimination, so I might as well connect the dots for him.

By the time we get to Lyon, Théo's up to speed enough to understand why it's so important to keep my secret. He has a million questions about the catacombs and Sébastien, but there's no time to cover everything. Besides, if we go into any more detail, I'd have to mention Gaspar, and I'm not ready to open that can of worms.

It's a rather warm day for late February. A few eager spring flowers are pushing their buds through the cold soil, reaching for the sun, which stands low in the sky. Théo points out some of the sights and historic buildings of Lyon as we head for the Cimetière de La Guillotière nouveau. Unlike the cemeteries of Paris with their rectangular avenues, this one's laid out in concentric circles, like a spider's web.

"How long has it been since you've been here?" I ask Théo as he finds his way through the different circle segments.

"I said goodbye when we left for Paris. There wasn't really any reason to go back, you know?"

"No friends?"

He chuckles. "Yeah, okay, I have some friends here, but most of us moved away, so it's kind of hard to get the whole gang together."

I catch myself thinking how good it'd be for Sébastien to be friends with Théo, now that they've had their little bonding experience. He could use a living guy who isn't socially handicapped.

"This is it," he says, with a heavy heart.

We've arrived at a part of the cemetery where plaques have replaced the expensive gravestones. The individual graves are small, so they can bury a lot of people here and save some space. As a result, it's a bit crowded.

"I forgot to tell you, we had them cremated. It was cheaper, you know, and Laurent thought it'd keep them together. Are they here?" His voice is suddenly small, a reminder of the little boy who lost his parents before he even reached puberty.

"Of course they're here." A pair of ghosts stand in front of us, looking so much like Théo, even though they look nothing like each other. He's got his mother's hair, nose, and chin, but his father's eyes and ears. "They look happy to see you."

Théo swallows, fighting back tears. "Can I just talk to them or...?"

I take his hand and nod. "You can just talk. I'll tell you what they... Just now your mum said she missed you." Actually, she said, "I've missed you, baby," but I don't want to embarrass Théo.

Gaby squeezes my arm before picking up Malou and taking her for a walk around the perimeter, keeping watch. Théo's crying now, but he's also smiling as we slowly find our groove in this three-way conversation. When he finally says goodbye, promising to come back more often, he's grinning from ear to ear. So are his parents, who thank me profusely for making this possible.

And I know then and there that I'll never let GoPol take this away from me. Now if that wasn't easier said than done.

CHAPTER 31

To thank us for taking care of Nat, Sébastien and I are invited back to the opera. But this time, it's to watch a ghost performance. Garnier welcomes us in the foyer and leads us to the best seats in the house. Thanks to Sébastien's badge and his contribution over the weekend, we have no trouble with the living staff. Most of them are at home sleeping, anyway.

It's another performance of Castor et Pollux, but this time it's Pélissier and Le Maure in the main female roles. To my surprise, they share the stage exceptionally well. Whether that's because the show is more important than their feud, or because Nat's hatred no longer affects them, I don't know. One thing's for sure, the ghosts are far superior to the living cast, especially the sopranos. They're not considered to be the greatest opera singers France has ever seen for nothing. Moreover, the setting is reminiscent of the period in which the play is set, without any contemporary director trying to leave his mark. I know, it's part of their art, but the history girl in me prefers the raw experience, unfiltered by a modern lens.

As we sit and listen to Telaira lament the second loss of her beloved, Sébastien puts a hand on mine and rubs his thumb over the burn mark on the side of my hand. "I never thanked you for that."

"You were busy arresting Nat."

He swallows but leaves his hand where it is. "It was necessary. She's already killed one person and tried to kill two"—his eyes wander to my unmarked neck—"three more."

"She only became like that because she felt left behind. Imagine, you die, and nobody cares. Instead, you see this mirror image of you, thriving and happy, while you're all alone. Maybe if we'd spent more time talking to her, we could have made it work for Natalie."

Sébastien lets go of my hand and takes a deep breath. "Would you say the same if Nat was still alive? One murder, three attempted murders, let's talk to them, see if they're okay?"

The embarrassing answer is, "No, of course not". Instead, I sigh. "I see what you mean, but we put murderers away; we don't kill them." At least not in this country.

Sébastien sighs, obviously still thinking the rules don't apply to ghosts. If anything, I'm of the opinion eliminating ghosts is worse than a death sentence. When you die, at least you've got the afterlife. If a ghost is taken out of this world, it's gone forever.

In a strained voice he says, "The danger these whisper ghosts pose—"

"Oh, don't give me that 'the end justifies all means' speech. What GoPol is doing is murder." I cross my arms and concentrate on the final act of the opera. "Plain and simple."

"It's the opposite of plain and simple," Sébastien complains quietly. "There are no laws about how to treat ghosts. They're not even recognised as people, which means, technically, it's not murder."

I wish I hadn't come across this argument a million times in the course of history class. People always justify their cruelty to themselves by dehumanising their victims. "Just because our current laws don't cover it adequately doesn't mean what we're doing is right. You know it's wrong. Otherwise, you wouldn't have come to me. Otherwise, you wouldn't care about Dix."

Dix is the magic word to get through to him. Sébastien slumps in his chair, clutches his hands, and stares blindly ahead. "I'm afraid, Alix," he admits after a while.

"Of what?"

"It feels like I'm on a slippery slope. I already ignored GoPol orders when it came to you. Objectively, you're like a huge security risk. And knowing you, hearing you talk, that risk is only growing."

"What do you think I'm going to do?" I ask, taken aback.

"If you don't die on me?" He looks at me. "Tear it all down."

That sounds at least three sizes too big for me, but I'm also strangely flattered. "And that terrifies you?"

"Doesn't it terrify you?"

"I'm afraid of people coming after me. Of being killed for the things I believe in, especially when all I want to do is help people. Not of painful or necessary change. Fear isn't a good enough reason to hold back." I put my hand on his. "We can't let the Charles Rouberts of this world go unchecked just because they're in power." I snort as an idea hits me. "If it helps, there's no law that says we have to destroy every whisper ghost that isn't attached to a GoPol agent, either. There's not a single law we can hide behind when it comes to ghosts, only our conscience."

He gives me a pained look. It reminds me of how willing Théo was to go all in. But he hardly knew what he was getting into, and he has no skin in the game. For Sébastien, it's the unravelling of a lifetime of being told otherwise. I know I've challenged his beliefs for him, but have I challenged them enough?

Only time will tell.

CHAPTER 32

O nce the opera has finished and we've applauded the ghost performers alongside the ghost subscribers, we make our way to the exit. We've just passed the backstage area when I hear the thump of EDM music again.

"Is that it?" Sébastien asks.

My head is already turned. The music beckons me. It fills me with all these emotions and yearning. Suddenly, I remember what Natalie told me. The Angel of Music is calling me. And I must follow.

"Alix!" Sébastien warns me, but I'm already on my way backstage.

Down some stairs. Down a corridor. Through a door. Down again. Now up. Behind a pillar. Climb up a ladder. Down two more levels. On and on the music calls.

"Alix!" Sébastien is somewhere behind me.

I can't slow down for him. It's as if the music has its own magic. I have to find out who's playing it, who's calling me, who wants me at their side.

Finally, I stumble into a cellar. In the middle of the room is a trapdoor with a metal grate. Below, I see the faint flicker of a torch reflected on a shimmering surface. Water.

I'm not surprised to find the grate unlocked. I open it carefully and climb down the steps. When my feet hit the ground, it's the uneven surface of raw stone. I've landed in a small cave with a pool of water in the sagging centre. The music sounds hollow here, which only adds to its haunting quality.

The torch appears to be around the corner, so I walk on the dry side until I reach it. A cave bigger than the stage stretches out before me. Everything is under water. The underground lake.

I'm back in the catacombs. Off to the side is a narrow walkway that seems to lead around the lake, but directly in front of me is a pier with a small boat tied to it. The distant light of another torch beckons me from across the lake. And the music, the music fills my ears.

The boat rocks a little as I get in, but before I can push off the pier, Sébastien arrives, out of breath. "What are you doing?"

"The music..." My heart yearns for it so much it aches. With pleading eyes, I look up at him, then past him.

My blood freezes.

Sébastien isn't alone. Behind him, coming around the corner, is no one else but the man who wants me dead.

C-Trente.

I stare just a moment too long before instinct kicks in and I look back at Sébastien. "Are you just going to stand there or will you join me?" As much as the music's calling me to the other side, I want to row away from this one.

Sébastien hesitates, but when he sees me grab the oar he jumps in. The boat rocks from side to side as he sits opposite me. "You don't know who's playing this music."

"The Angel of Music, of course," I reply, trying to keep my voice light. By now I've found the second oar and am pushing away from the pier.

Now, I'm no rowing expert. In fact, I've only done it once or twice on a summer holiday where the aim was to play in the boat rather than get anywhere. The first time I put the oars in, it's so deep I can't pull them through. One oar gives after a moment, but the other just flails in the air, splashing Sébastien with water. Maybe I'm also a little too nervous.

"Let me do it," he offers, already moving to switch places with me.

Every instinct in my body tells me to stay seated so I don't have to get any closer to C-Trente, but I tell my overworked nerves that we'll get away quicker if I let Sébastien do the hard work.

As I feel C-Trente breathing down my neck, Sébastien turns around. His eyes widen as he recognises the whisper ghost. "Alix, don't freak out," he says in a tense voice. At the same moment, he pulls on the oars, and we take a giant leap onto the lake. Thank goodness for his workouts.

"C-Trente followed us," he says, as if I didn't know that with every nerve in my body. He shouts at the ghost: "I told you to leave her alone."

"What's he doing?" I ask, turning my head to pretend I'm looking for him. "Where is he?" My voice is so shaky I don't know if it's helping or betraying me.

I know damn well where he is. Although I try not to look directly at him, I can see him coming towards us. It doesn't matter that there's water between us. Normal rules don't apply to C-Trente and he walks across the water as if it were a solid surface.

"Behind us," Sébastien mumbles. "Hey, C! If you don't turn back now, I'll have to report you."

"To whom?" C-Trente says amused. "Have you forgotten who holds your leash?"

"Leash?" Sébastien repeats, horrified. A few more strokes and we're in the middle of the lake. "I'm not a dog on a leash."

My fingers dig into the wood of the bench below me. My shoulders are so tense I'm afraid I won't be able to unlock them once we're out of here, while my gaze is fixed on the flickering torch on the other side, willing the shore to us.

"That's what you are," C-Trente says. "You're supposed to be your father's dog. Instead, you're running after this bitch."

"Excuse me? She's my *girlfriend*."

C-Trente scoffs. "Oh, forgive me, I forgot about your so-called act; you pretending to love her so you can keep an eye on her." Sébastien says nothing, which makes the words only cut deeper. "If that were truly the case, why didn't you tell us she was still one of us?"

"Because she's not." Sébastien looks over his shoulder, estimating how much longer he'll have to row. "She's lost her ability."

"Is he questioning that?" I ask in a feeble attempt to assist him. "I haven't seen a ghost in months."

"Oh yeah?" C-Trente asks. "Then how come you've surrounded yourself with opera ghosts and fought off a whisper ghost? The whole building is buzzing about your pitiful heroics."

Splinters ding into the soft flesh under my nails as I grab the wood of the bench harder. But I don't say a word, because I'm not supposed to have heard anything. "We're almost there," I tell Sébastien instead. The opposite bank is so close.

C-Trente snorts. "I don't believe you, little girl, and as for you," he clearly means Sébastien, "I'll be the one to report *you*. You were supposed to exterminate her whisper ghost like the good little dog you are."

Sébastien's face distorts in anger. "I did! She can't see you!"

Suddenly, C-Trente's voice is right behind me. "Turn around for me, Alix."

I resist the urge to jump out of the boat.

"She can't hear you, either," Sébastien says, seemingly annoyed. His voice is shaking, though, ruining the act. He lifts one of the oars instead of continuing to row.

"Then I guess she can't feel my touch either."

When his hands land on my shoulder, I know my performance is hanging by a thread. It takes sheer willpower to keep my shoulders relaxed. I even let go of the bench.

"Don't touch her," Sébastien snarls. He stands up and grips the oar with both hands.

"Why not? She's lost her ability, right? So she won't feel it when I do this."

Before I can ask myself what terrible thing he has planned for me, I'm tossed from the boat into the lake.

CHAPTER 33

The cold shocks me. Then panic hits me. I was already nervous as hell and now I've been plunged into my worst nightmare. Never mind that my act has just officially been torn apart.

My feet hit the ground and for a moment I feel hopeful I'll make it out. We aren't that far from the shore, but just as my head is about to burst through the surface, C-Trente's ghastly face appears in front of me.

He spins me around, pinning my body to his as he holds my head underwater. "You die here."

I thrash and kick, my lungs struggling for air, but C-Trente is much stronger than me and he doesn't seem to have any buoyancy. Instead, we stay at the bottom of the lake, his arms so tight around my chest it squeezes the last of the air out of me.

My cheeks burn from holding a pocket of air in my mouth, as if it would do me any good there. My lungs begin to prickle as if stung by a thousand needles. The need for air becomes over-whelming.

"See you on the other side, little one," C-Trente whispers in my ear, filling me with more fear and terror.

I want to scream, but that would defeat the purpose of keeping my mouth shut. Everything hurts, my mouth, my lungs, and now my head, too. My body needs oxygen and if I don't get it in a minute or less, I'll die at the bottom of this lake.

Just then C-Trente moans. The pressure on my chest eases. Just a little at first, then his arms let go completely.

Now would be the perfect time to push off and break through the surface, but I can't feel the ground beneath me. I don't even know if it *is* underneath me. I twist and turn, not sure if I'm swimming for the bottom, the surface, or deeper into the lake. My lungs are now screaming for air. My lips beckon me to open them. Surely I can breathe water, can't I?

A hand grabs my arm and hauls me onto a hard, unforgiving surface. My mouth opens on impact, and I gasp. I expect water to rush in, but instead air fills my lungs. Sweet, musty air.

I turn around and cough, as if that'll relieve the burning sensation in my throat.

Before I have time to take in my surroundings, something heavy slams into me, forcing the air out of my lungs again. Fingers wrap around my neck, and someone slams my head into the stone beneath me.

I don't know whether to focus on the squeezing fingers, the explosion of pain on my forehead, or the crushing weight on my body.

"She can't feel this," C-Trente's sick voice rejoices. "She can't feel any of this, can she?"

My head is slammed into the stone again and I feel my consciousness slip away for a moment.

A shot is fired. Then another and another. Shot after shot echoes through the cave until the weight on my body is lifted and the pressure around my neck is gone. I taste blood in my mouth as my back is pelted with... grains.

It feels like I'm being showered with sand. Yet I can clearly hear a gun going off again and again.

When I finally manage to roll onto my back, I see Sébastien standing over me, legs spread, gun in both hands, sheer determination on his face. He fires again, but I can't see what he's shooting at. C-Trente has already disappeared.

Sébastien reloads, but there's just an empty click. Tired, his arm drops, and the gun falls to the ground. A second later, his knees hit the stone. "He's gone."

It's not until I taste the salt in my blood that I realise what he's done. "You destroyed him."

Sébastien stares at me with a haunted look in his eyes. Then suddenly he lunges forward, grabs my shoulders, and presses me against his chest. "You're alive. You're alive."

His relief washes over me as my body regains sensation. I tremble in his painful embrace, yet I never want him to let go of me again. "Is it true?" I ask doubtfully. "He didn't just disappear. You actually destroyed him?"

"I shot so many rounds of salt into him, there's no way he'll ever reform." He's got one arm around my back and the other pressed against my head. "I thought I'd lost you."

"I'm still here," I say, reassuring not only him but myself as well. "You saved me," I repeat, still in awe. "You killed your father for me."

"If only."

I stare at him, stunned. Did he really just say that? "Sébastien?"

His piercing blue eyes meet mine. "I'm yours, Alix. I'm all yours. You scare the living shit out of me, but I'd follow you to the ends of the earth. I would."

Astonished, I reach for his cheek. There's a bruise on his temple and blood in his hair from the fight with C-Trente. But Sébastien prevailed. He's gone completely rogue for me.

My thumb brushes over where his lip is split. The heat of his breath warms my skin. "Thanks," I whisper.

His eyes drop to my lips and as he moves towards me, my hand slips around his neck, pulling him closer.

Salt and the metallic taste of blood mix as our mouths meet, but it's quickly washed away by the heat of his tongue between my lips and the pressure of his body against mine. I drink him in as if I were still drowning and he's the air I need to breathe. Our shared loss and common enemy bind us tighter together than our arms could ever do.

I have no idea what it means, but it feels good. I feel safe and loved and—

A slow clap behind us makes us both jump. "How moving," says a voice, dripping with contempt.

The man standing behind Sébastien is the one I'd hoped to find, yet least expected after all this time. With black fingernails, floppy brown hair, but not a hint of warmth in his eyes, Gaspar's contemptuous stare meets my eyes.

"Good to know you haven't forgotten me."

Afterword

How much fun was it to dive into the opera? Did you get all the references to *The Phantom of the Opera*? When I read Leroux's book in preparation, I was amazed at how neatly it would reflect the relationships in Parisian Ghosts. With Gaspar (and Nat) as the Phantom and Alix as Christine, Sébastien had to take on the role of a more competent, less whiny Raoul. Or maybe that was Théo. Speaking of Théo, I like the way Alix's little gang is growing. And of course, they all have to swear by Malou.

While Alix has had to cope without Gaspar in this book, she accidentally grew closer to Sébastien in the process. I never thought I'd write a fake-dating trope, but the situation just lent itself to it. Don't worry, contrary to what he said, Gaspar is not forgotten.

At the heart of this instalment, though, is the relationship between the sisters. As much as I loved writing the big intervention from a dramatic perspective, it also tore my heart out. Poor Alix has so many obstacles to overcome, and for a moment it looked like she was ready to give up on Hélène. In the end, the relationship between Natalie and Emanuelle inspired her to reach out again. Family, right. Can't live with them or without them, although I'm a little worried about whether Alix compromised too much to achieve that peace. I guess we'll have to see in the next book when it's finally time for Hélène and Cédric's wedding. Will it go off without a hitch? Not when ghosts are involved.

But first, Alix has to figure out this new development in her love life. With both Gaspar and Sébastien vying for her love, the next book is sure to be explosive. Who's she gonna pick, or is she going with Marie's suggestion and taking them both?

I'd like to thank Isa who sat down with me for tea and scones as I tried to figure out how to stage the murder, Perri who came up with the motto for Gaspar's family crypt, and Jackie who, as always, supported my process, filled my writing nights with chatter, and had the audacity to call me in the middle of writing the kissing scene! How rude!

Also, a huge thank you to my beta readers Paula, Tina, and Jojo for standing by to dissect the book, despite my late delivery. This book would never have made it in time without your quick and careful work.

Last but not least, thank you to my children, who have finally understood what it means when Mummy is in the flow, and to my ever-supportive husband.

Now pack your bags, we're leaving Paris for the south of France!

Love, Janna

The adventure continues...

Book 5: Ghosts of the Provence

A Force of Nature (Spirit Seeker 1)

A supernatural adventure through Europe

A Drop of Magic (Ashuan Greed 1)

Magic, Demons and High School Drama

About Janna Ruth

Once upon a time, Janna Ruth studied the plate boundaries of this world. Now, she's creating her own worlds. Born in Berlin, Germany, Janna lives in Wellington, New Zealand, writing both English and German books.

Janna's writing career kicked off when she won a writing competition for German publisher Ueberreuter. Her first self-published novel "Im Bann der zertanzten Schuhe" (Melody of Curse, coming in June 2022) went on to win the 2018 SERAPH for "Best Independent Title". She debuted in English with her witchy novella "Witching with Dolphins" in 2020 and has since published urban fantasy, YA sci-fi, and contemporary coming-of-age novels and series.

When Janna isn't writing, she has a plethora of hobbies, such as aerial acrobatics, cake decorating, drawing, reading, and anything crafty you can throw her way.

Find out more about Janna and her books here:

- **Website:** www.janna-ruth.com

- **BookBub:** www.bookbub.com/authors/janna-ruth

- **Facebook:** www.facebook.com/authorjannaruth

- **Facebook Reader Group:** www.facebook.com/groups /storyseekers

- **Twitter:** www.twitter.com/jannaRuthAuthor

- **Instagram:** www.instagram.com/janna_ruth

- **TikTok:** www.tiktok.com/@jannaruthwrites

- **Pinterest:** www.pinterest.com/jannaruthwrites

www.ingramcontent.com/pod-product-compliance
Lightning Source LLC
Chambersburg PA
CBHW031057130726
47906CB00008B/751